UGLY CAT & Pablo

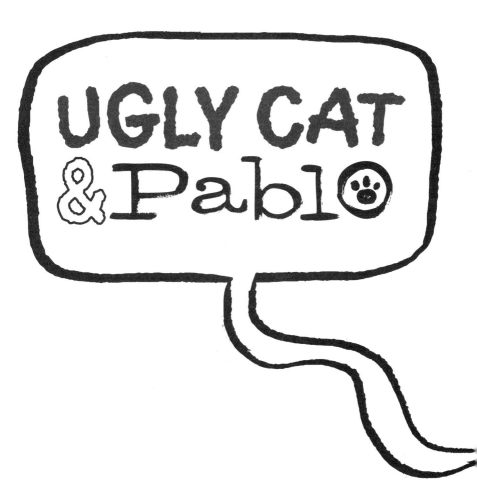

Isabel
Quintero

With illustrations by

Tom Knight

Scholastic Press

This book is being published simultaneously in paperback by Scholastic Inc.

All rights reserved. Published by Scholastic Press, an imprint of Scholastic Inc., *Publishers since 1920.* SCHOLASTIC, SCHOLASTIC PRESS, and associated logos are trademarks and/or registered trademarks of Scholastic Inc.

The publisher does not have any control over and does not assume any responsibility for author or third-party websites or their content.

This book is a work of fiction. Names, characters, places, and incidents are either the product of the author's imagination or are used fictitiously, and any resemblance to actual persons, living or dead, business establishments, events, or locales is entirely coincidental.

Library of Congress Cataloging-in-Publication Data available

ISBN 978-0-545-94092-4

10 9 8 7 6 5 4 3 2 1   17 18 19 20 21

Printed in the U.S.A.   160
First edition, May 2017

Book design by Nina Goffi

Para todos los paleteros who make summers better

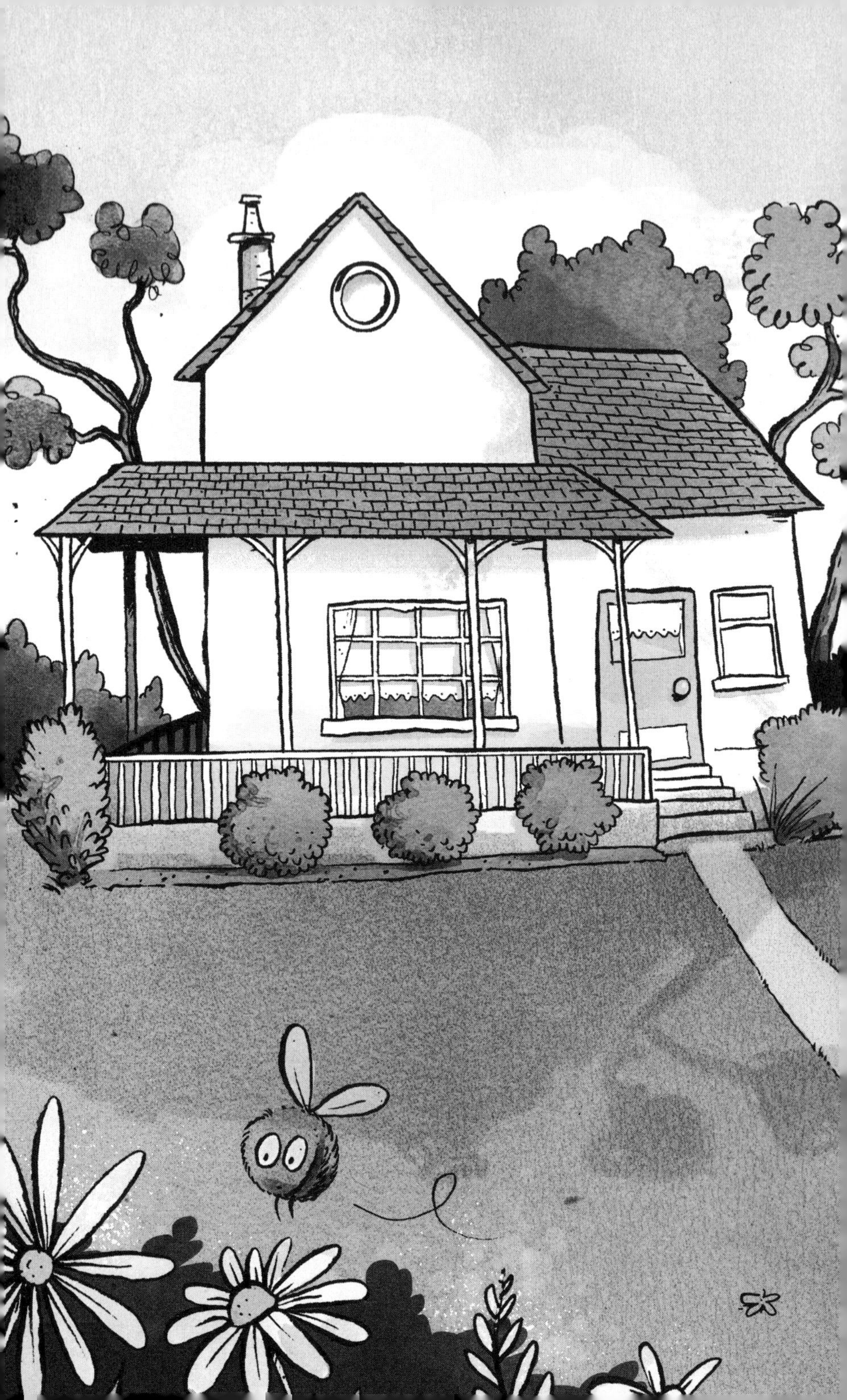

CHAPTER ONE

The Great, Glorious Idea

Pablo woke up feeling adventure in his itty-bitty mouse bones. He threw on his vest and hat and hurried out the door toward his best friend's house.

The closer Pablo got to Ugly Cat's house, the more he began to daydream about what kind of adventures they would have. He saw Ugly and himself as ghost hunters, exploring the old Herrera house way at the edge of the neighborhood, where the streets stopped and the forest began. They'd go in with flashlights, carefully searching closets, tiptoeing up to the second floor. Ugly Cat would hear a low creak behind a door, and Pablo would take a look (because, of course, he'd be much braver), and then suddenly—

BEEP!

The horn of the Mendozas' blue minivan brought Pablo out of his daydream.

"Oh, mi barriguita!" he said, clutching his stomach. "I almost lost my lasagna!" Pablo shook his fist at the minivan that whipped around the corner. He caught his breath and then kept walking.

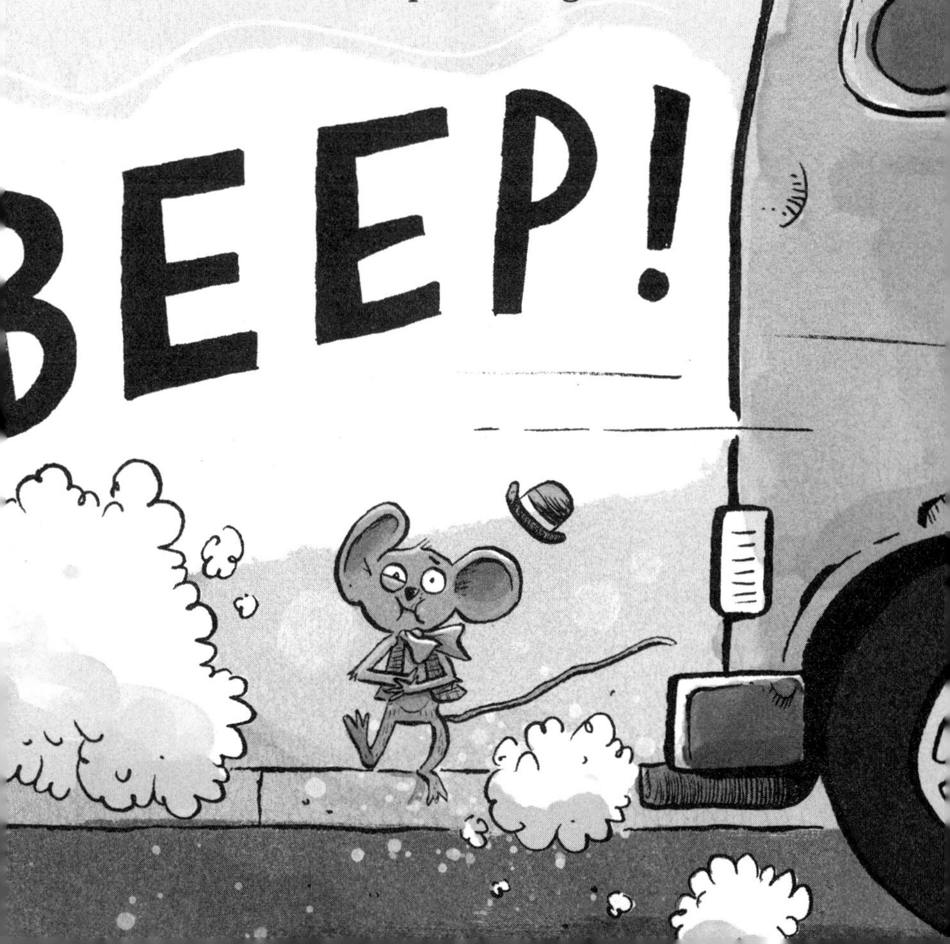
BEEP!

When Pablo reached Ugly Cat's house, he bounded up the steps and discovered Ugly Cat lying on the porch stretching, yawning, and soaking in the sun. He was in one of those I'm-too-lazy-to-move-let's-just-look-at-the-clouds kind of moods.

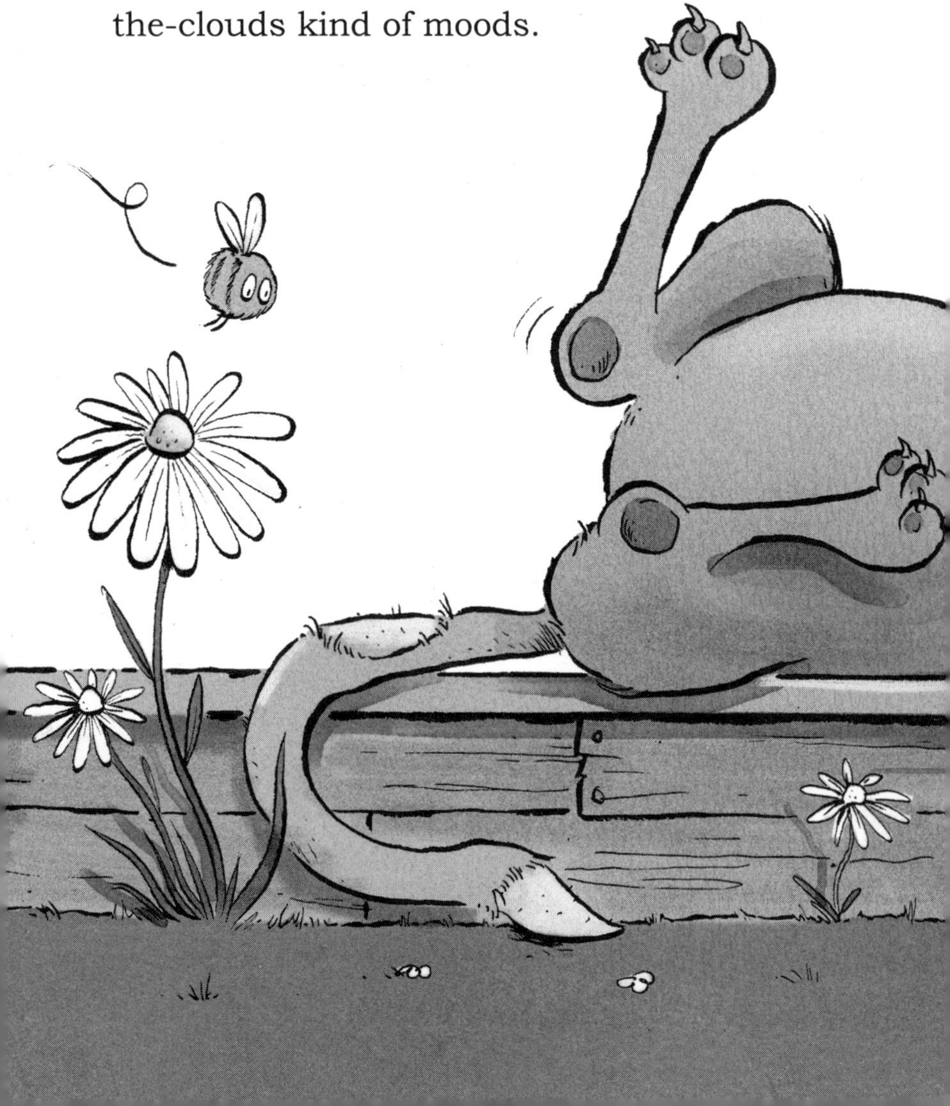

"Ugly! Come on! We need to do something today. We can't just lie around doing nothin'."

Pablo pleaded with his best friend.

Ugly Cat just looked at him and stuck his tongue out toward his water bowl. He was thirsty but not thirsty enough to get up.

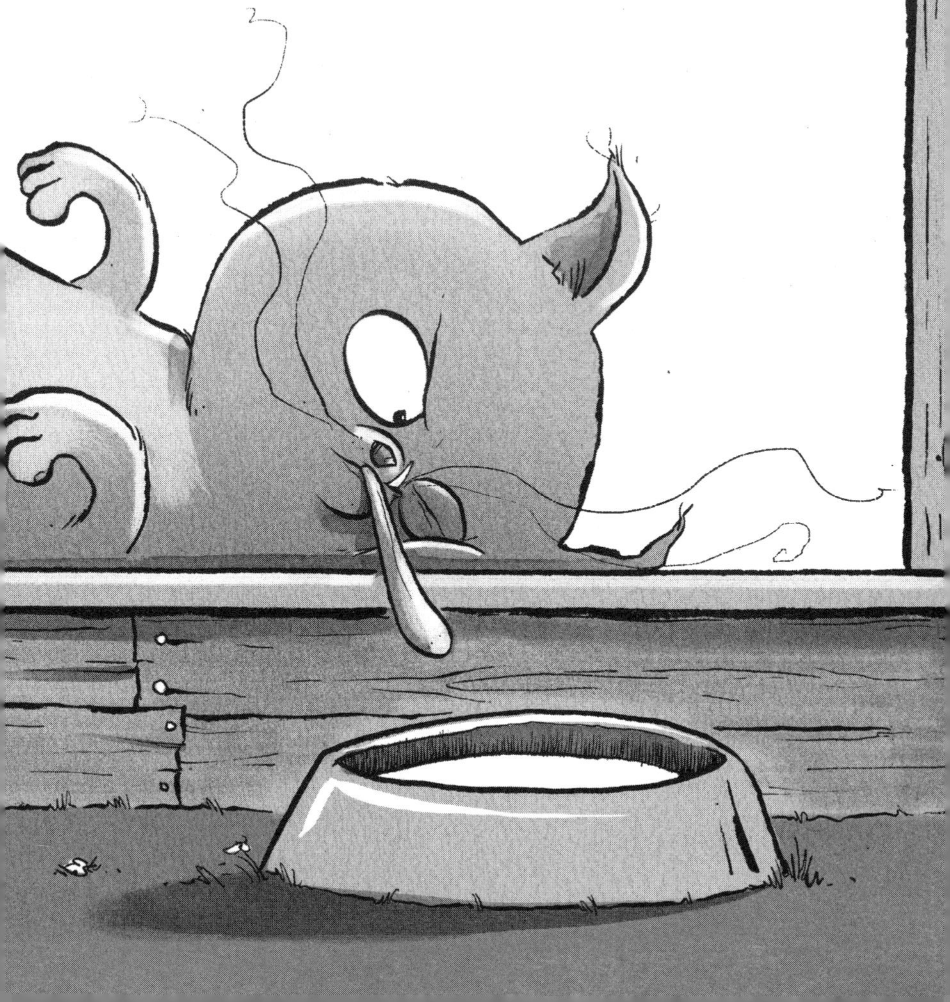

Pablo kept at it until Ugly Cat finally gave in. **"OKAY, PABLO. WHAT SHOULD WE DO TODAY?"** Ugly Cat asked, licking and examining his claws. **"YOU WANNA PLAY WITH BIG MIKE AGAIN?"**

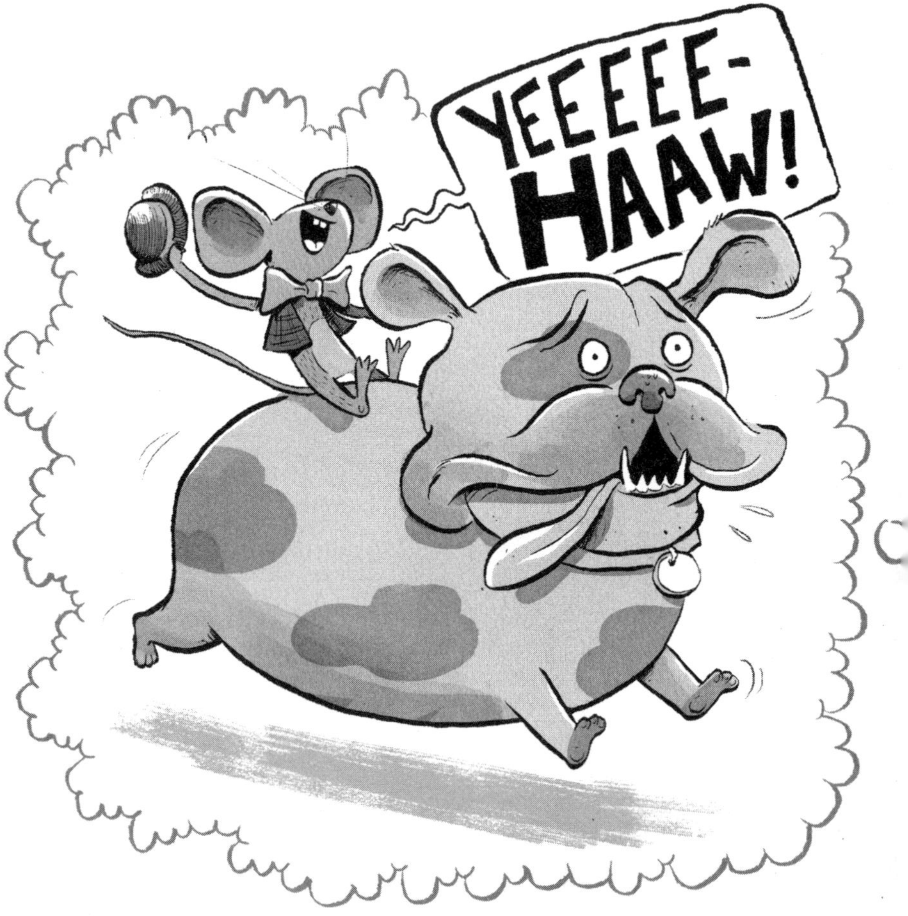
YEEEEE-
HAAW!

Big Mike, a stout English bulldog, lived behind Ugly Cat's house. The day before, Ugly Cat and Pablo had chased Big Mike all around his yard. Ugly Cat had blocked Big Mike from getting back inside his house, while Pablo jumped on his back and rode that poor dog like he was an angry bull at a rodeo.

Big Mike hadn't talked to them since.

"Tempting, but no. Big Mike seemed really hurt when I walked by there earlier," said Pablo. He couldn't look Ugly Cat in the eye because he knew they had really messed up the day before, though neither of them wanted to admit it.

The thing was that Big Mike, who was a really good friend, hadn't had a fun time. At all. Big Mike actually had a horrible, I-can't-believe-my-friends-would-do-this-to-me time. Ugly Cat and Pablo knew they had taken advantage of him, they knew that friends were not mean to each other, and they definitely knew that friends don't ride friends like bulls, especially when the other friend said he didn't want to play rodeo and had asked them to stop. They had broken all those friendship rules, and now they didn't know what to do or how to talk about it. So they tried ignoring it, but it was really hard to do.

Ugly Cat broke the uncomfortable silence.

"WELL, WE COULD TRY AND SCARE CHRISTY, FROM UP THE BLOCK. YOU KNOW THAT LADY WHO TOLD LILY TO NAME ME UGLY CAT BECAUSE SHE THOUGHT I WAS SOOO UGLY? I STILL CAN'T BELIEVE THAT LILY LISTENED TO HER. I MEAN, REALLY . . .

COME ON! HOW COULD ANYONE THINK I AM UGLY? UN GATO TAN GUAPO COMO YO? LOOK AT ME! LOOK AT THIS FACE! THIS IS THE FACE OF A HEARTBREAKER!"

Few things got Ugly Cat up from an afternoon of lazing around. One of them was showing off how beautiful he was. He jumped up and began striking poses. Then he pranced around a bit so Pablo could see him in all his splendor.

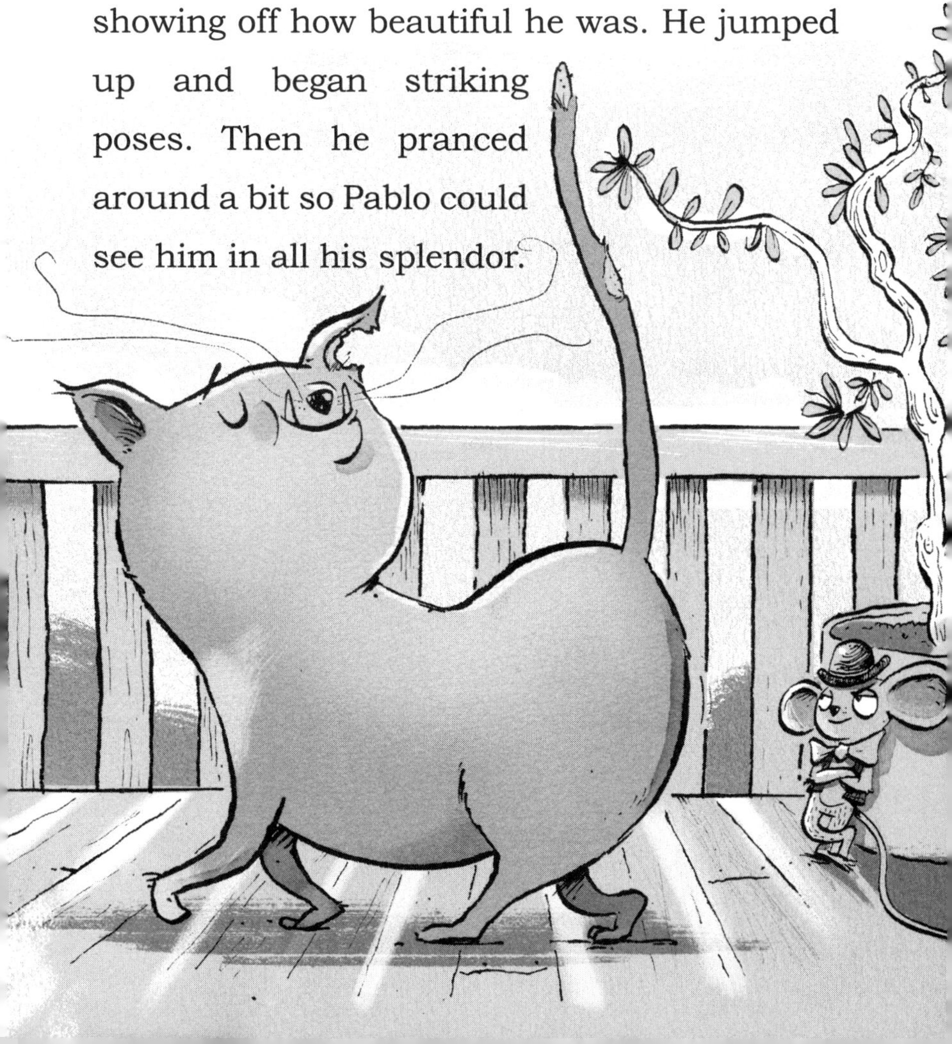

"Yeah, maybe," said Pablo, eyeing Ugly Cat's balding tail and missing piece of ear. "Let's try to think of something else."

Pablo thought of more things to do, but Ugly Cat didn't like any of his suggestions. When Pablo brought up the old Herrera house, Ugly Cat gave a little yelp and shook his head. Then Pablo came up with a great, glorious idea.

"I've got it! Mi querido Feo, vámonos al parque! You know we always have fun there." Ugly Cat's eyes widened, and he couldn't stop nodding as Pablo went on. "There'll be all sorts of people stuffing their faces! Remember last week when we went and you nipped that little kid on the ankle and he dropped his ice cream? That wasn't nice, so we shouldn't do that, but, oh my galleta, it was delicious! This time maybe we could keep our teeth and claws to ourselves? I mean, it was a good tactic, but we wouldn't want to get banned from the park. Then we couldn't have any treats. You know? Ugly? You listening?"

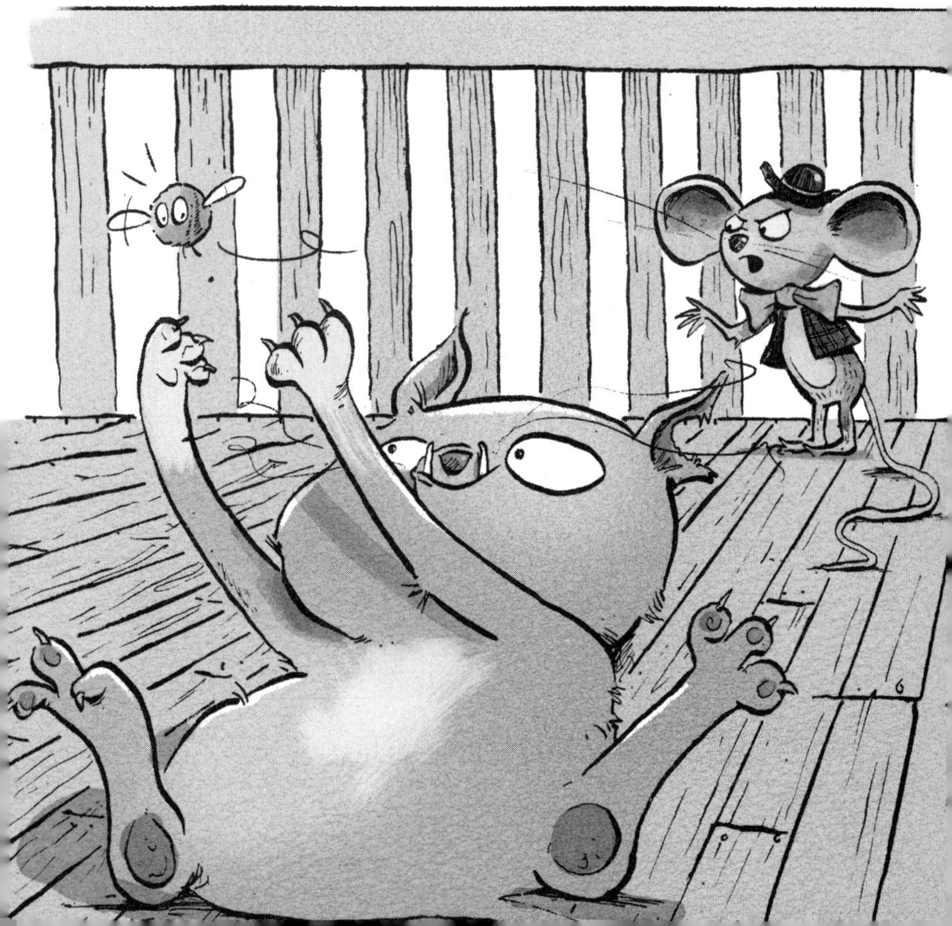

Ugly Cat was kind of listening, but also kind of daydreaming about all the food there would be at the park. Ugly Cat daydreamed about food like Pablo daydreamed about adventure.

"YEAH!" Ugly Cat said as he licked his whiskers, drool dripping from his mouth. **"HOW COULD I FORGET? I WAS ALL LIKE, 'REEEEEWR,' AND THEN I GAVE HIM A NIBBLE ON THE ANKLE! AND THEN THE LITTLE KID WAS LIKE, 'AH!' AND HE DROPPED THE ICE-CREAM CONE AND WE WERE LIKE, 'YUM!' AND, AW MAN, IT WAS SOOOO GOOD! HA!"**

Ugly Cat looked at Pablo, who was giving him a no-biting-anyone-for-reals look, and said, **"DON'T WORRY, I WON'T BITE ANYONE. SHEESH. BUT LET'S HURRY AND FIND US A FOOD-DROPPING CHUMP BEFORE THE GOODIES ARE ALL GONE!"**

Ugly Cat and Pablo jumped off the front porch steps.

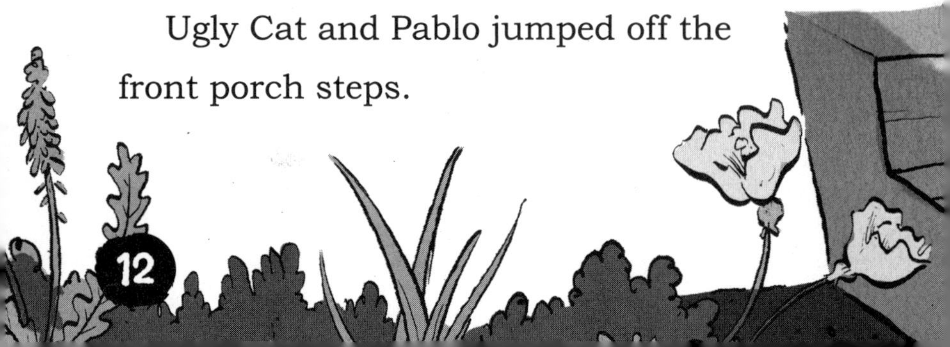

"Yes!" Pablo said. "Who better than us to make someone lose their lunch? Maybe an old man will drop a hot dog or maybe even, if we're lucky, a Polish sausage!"

Ugly Cat looked over at Pablo and exclaimed,

"GAH! I LOVE POLISH SAUSAGES!"

With that, the two friends took off straight to el parque faster than their friend Eric the weasel after a chicken.

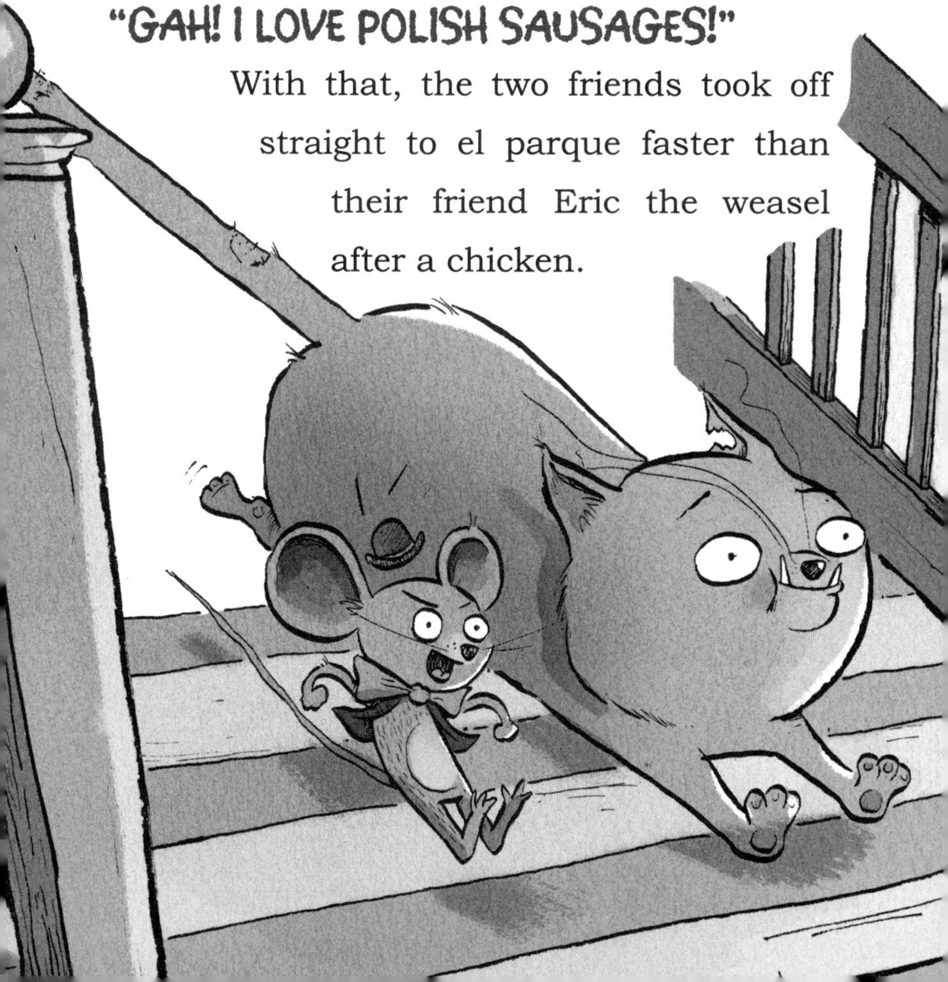

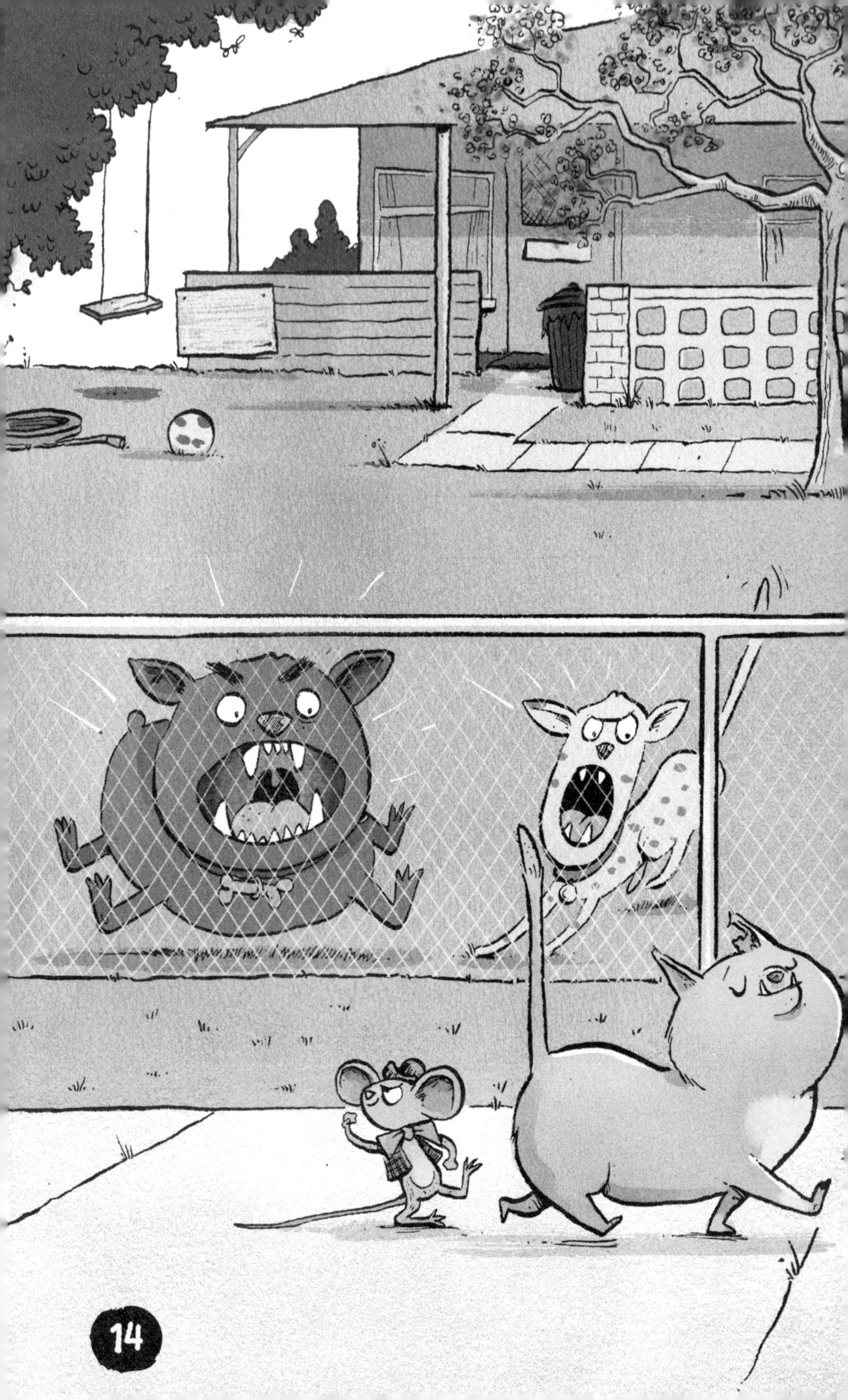

CHAPTER TWO

A Heavenly Vision

Ugly Cat and Pablo rushed up Longaniza Court, down Gordita Way, and around the corner of Tapatío Street to the park. The neighborhood dogs barked at them from behind the fence.

Pablo shook his fist at the pestering pooches. "Keep barking, you miserable mutts! You're only acting tough because you're on the other side of the fence and you know we're in a hurry for some fantastic franks! Or else we'd really let you have it!"

Pablo was never afraid of any dog, no matter how big they might be.

Well, maybe he was a teensy, tiny bit cautious of Cleopatra. But then again, who wouldn't be? Cleopatra was a miniature Doberman pinscher who lived across the street from Pablo and ruled the street with a heart of gold but an iron fist. She was a beast.

"YEAH! JUST WAIT TILL WE GET OUR SAUSAGEY NUTRIENTS. WE'LL COME BACK, AND THEN WE'LL SEE WHO BARKS LAST!" Ugly Cat shouted, forgetting that cats don't bark.

Finally, after a long and very loud walk, the two comrades arrived at the park. And boy, were they in luck. It was packed. A festival was set up right in the middle, and food vendors were everywhere. Each selling their specialty: burritos, gyros, tamales, churros, hamburgers, hot dogs, raspados, and chicharrones. Ugly Cat and Pablo followed the delicious aromas all around the fair, leaving a long slobbery trail of drool behind them. They danced toward the hot dog stand, singing, **"SAL-CHI-CHAS! Sal-chi-chas! DELiCiOUS LiTTLE HOT DOGS iN OUR BELLiES!"**

Then they saw . . . **THE CART**. They immediately became so enchanted with its beauty that they stopped singing.

The cart was as splendid and spectacular as the sun. The beautiful thing almost blinded passersby with its incandescence. The majestic cart, with the hypnotizing little bells that were like a siren's song that Ugly Cat especially couldn't resist, sat underneath the shade of a giant oak tree. That little cart and its bells could only mean one wonderfully delicious thing: paletas. Sweet, cold, otherworldly, fruity, and creamy paletas. Paletas were undoubtedly Ugly Cat's most favorite treat, and whenever there was one in sight, he had to have one or he would surely die.

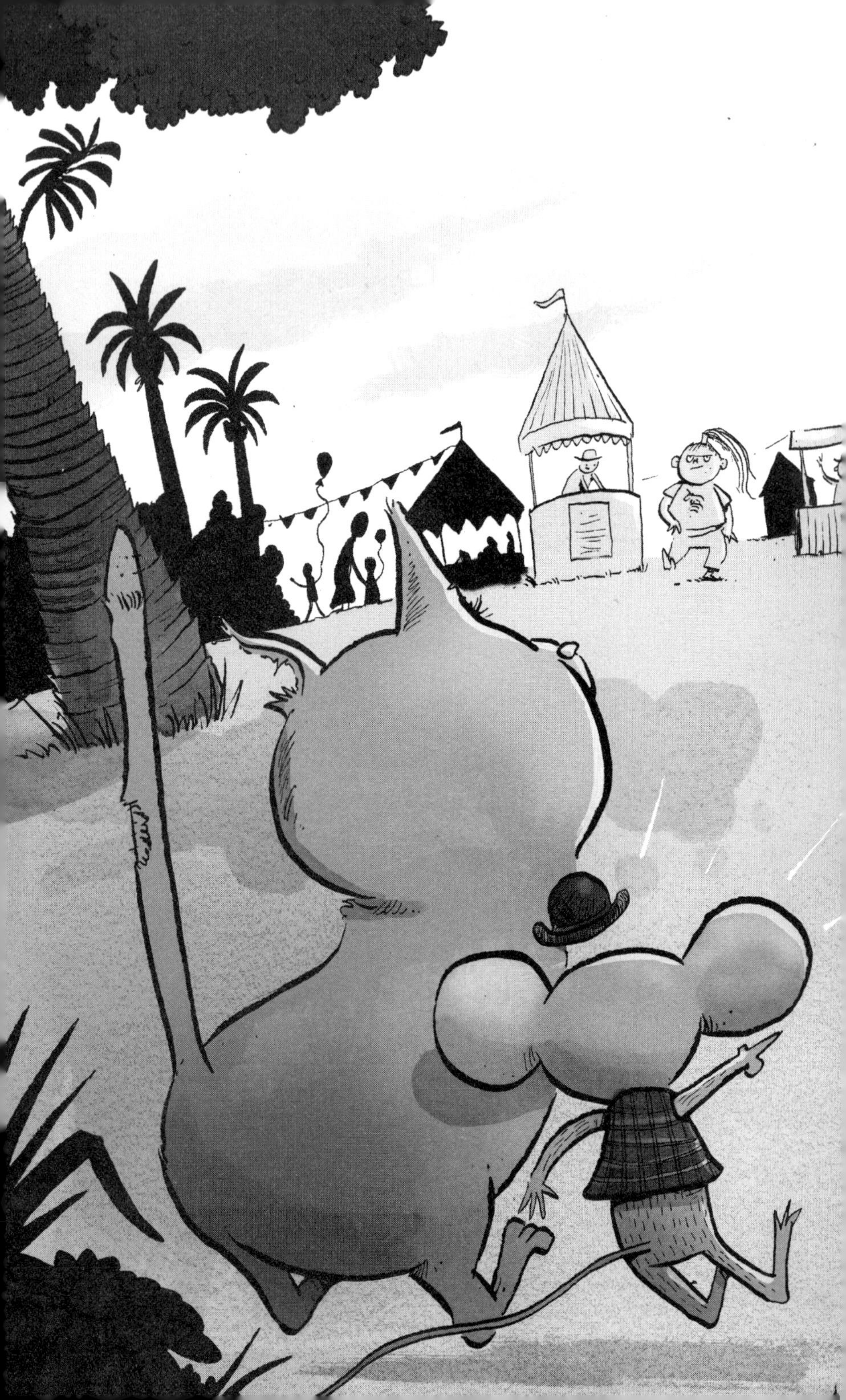

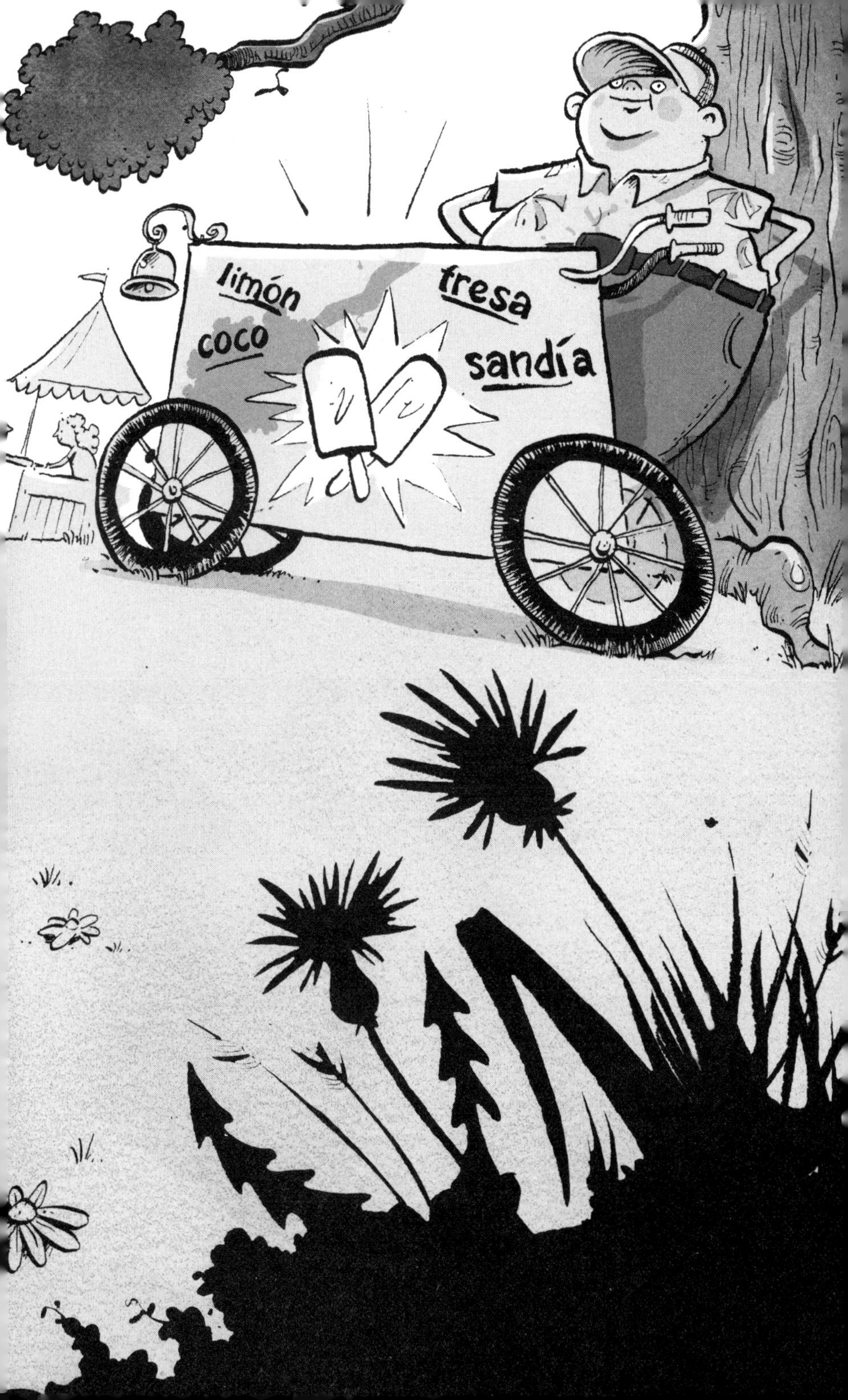
limón
fresa
coco
sandía

"PALETAS! PALETAS! PALETAS!" Ugly Cat started jumping up and down, hopping from one foot to the other. "I HAVE TO HAVE ONE, PABLO. IF I DON'T GET ONE, I WILL SURELY DIE. I JUST KNOW IT."

Pablo rolled his eyes and turned to admire a dandelion.

Ugly Cat tried harder. "AHHH! I'M DYING, PABLO! IN FACT, I SEE A LIGHT, I SEE A LIGHT! I THINK IT'S GATO HEAVEN! YES, THERE'S MY ABUELA PETUNIA AND PRIMO TOM. WHAT'S

THAT, TÍO JERRY? I DIED BECAUSE I DIDN'T EAT A PALETA? I KNEW IT!" Ugly Cat turned and implored Pablo, who was pretending to ignore him. "YOU HEAR THAT, PABLITO? HOW CAN WE ARGUE WITH THE DEAD? OUR ANCESTORS KNOW! THEY KNOW THAT THE ONLY WAY TO SAVE ME IS TO GET A PALETA! HELP ME, PABLO!"

By this point, Ugly Cat was lying on his belly looking up at Pablo, his paws clasped and pleading.

"You and your paletas!" scoffed Pablo, who acted as if he were going to walk away.

Ugly Cat couldn't believe it. "PABLO," he whispered, his paw outstretched toward his friend.

Pablo immediately turned around and grabbed Ugly Cat's big orange face with his small gray paws. "I'm just kidding! How can I look into those puppy-dog eyes and say no?"

"PABLO, YOU'RE THE BEST FRIEND A HANDSOME CAT LIKE ME COULD EVER ASK FOR!" Then Ugly Cat got nervous and began to bite his claws. "BUT HOW? HOW?! THAT LITTLE GIRL IS BUYING A COCONUT PALETA, AND WHAT IF SHE BUYS ALL OF THEM AND THEN THERE AREN'T ANY MORE LEFT FOR US? NO MORE PALETAS?! WE DON'T EVEN HAVE ANY MONEY!"

The cat began to frantically scratch his head with his paws, making fur fly. "AND IF WE DID HAVE MONEY, WHERE WOULD WE PUT IT? I DON'T HAVE POCKETS! DO YOU HAVE ANY? NO, YOU DON'T BECAUSE THOSE POCKETS ON YOUR VEST ARE FAKE! FAKE POCKETS THAT DON'T OPEN! WHY

Do they put fake pockets on things? I hate fake pockets! And without pockets, where would we put all this money that we don't have? Pablito, Pablito, how can we live like this?" Ugly Cat threw himself on the sidewalk.

Pablo just rolled his eyes at his feline friend. He had seen him much worse than this when the paleta cart at the swap meet had run out and was never refilled. That time Ugly Cat really went berserk.

"Let me think, Ugly Cat! Sheesh, don't get your tail in a knot. Pick yourself up, and wipe those mocos away. You look a mess. And fix your bow! Let's think how we can solve this problem." He tapped his chin as he thought, Hmmmm. Paletas, paletas, paletas. Hmmmm.

Pablo's eyes began to twitch and twinkle. And Ugly Cat knew—an idea was coming.

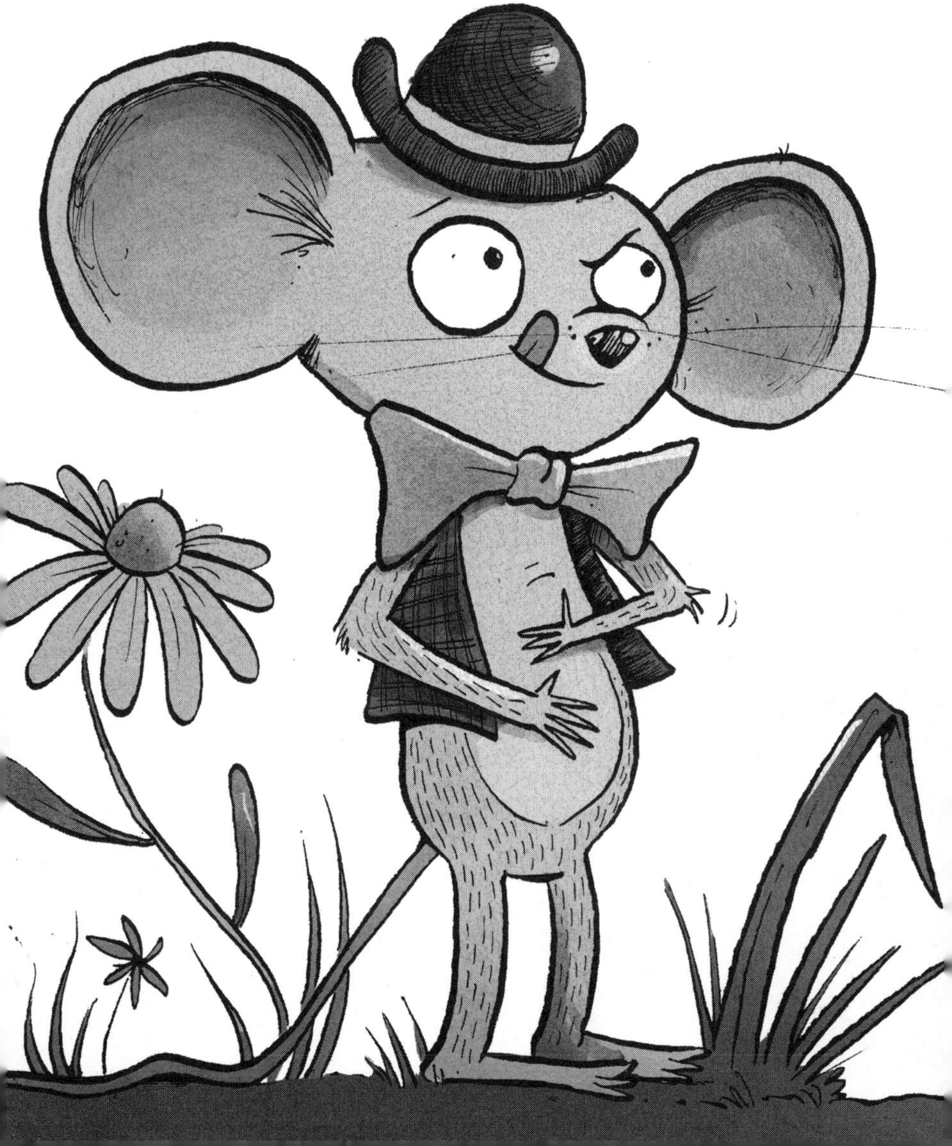

CHAPTER THREE

The Fool-Proof Plan

Every time Pablo devised a plan, it was the same thing. He would scratch his head, and then he would rub his belly. Then, when the idea was getting really good, he'd take his paws and place them behind his back and sniff the air. Lastly, he'd twitch his tail and clap his paws. This ritual was the sign of true genius. He had used this fool-proof method many times before.

Pablo clapped his paws and began to speak. "Here's what we'll do," he said. "Everyone knows that little girls are scared of mice, right?"

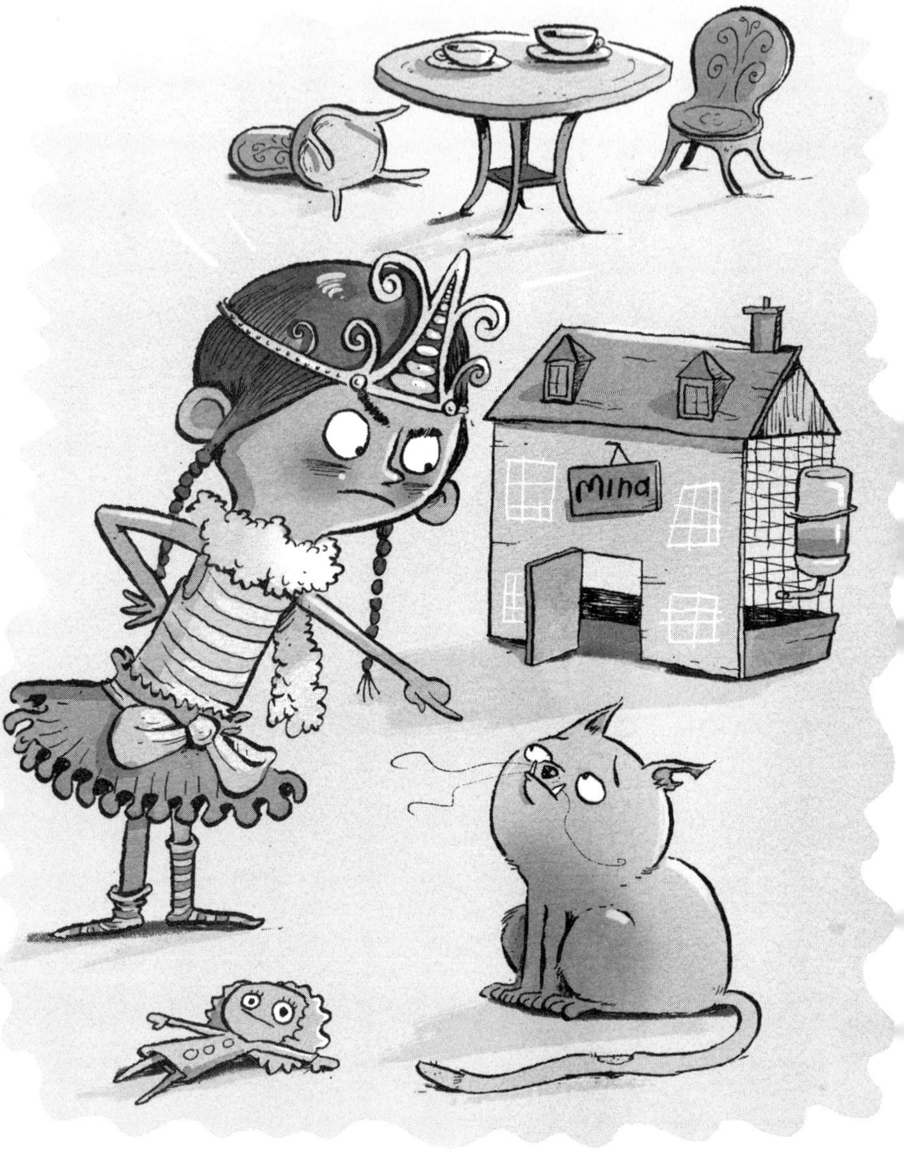
Mina

Ugly Cat shook his head because he didn't think that was true: He'd seen plenty of little girls playing with mice and rats and guinea pigs and even (shudder) tarantulas. In fact, Lily had a pet mouse, Mina, for a very short time, a few months back. One day, Mina just escaped and disappeared forever. Lily blamed Ugly Cat, but she could never find any proof that he'd committed a crime.

Pablo was so worked up that he ignored his friend. "It will be easy peasy lemon squeezy. You, my ferocious feline, will jump on the cart, scaring the cream out of the ice-cream man. You know, doing the ol' hissing and scratching routine." Pablo then jumped around, hissing and scratching in Ugly Cat's direction. He had completely forgotten about the part where he said he didn't want them to get kicked out of the park.

"And then I will creepy-crawl up Little Miss Paleta de Coco's leg. She'll be so terrified that she'll scream, 'Oh no! It's the most frightening mouse I have ever seen! Ahhhh!' And she'll drop not only the coconutty treat, but the chicharrones that she's carrying as well. Y listo, mi querido Feo, you will be in paleta heaven in no time. Or my name isn't..."

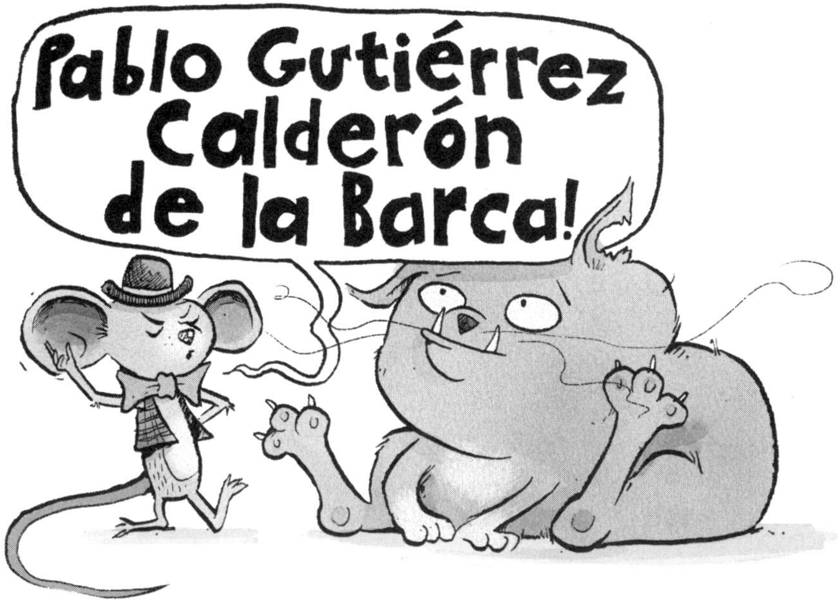
Pablo Gutiérrez Calderón de la Barca!

Ugly Cat looked surprised. "YOUR NAME IS PABLO GUTIÉRREZ CALDERÓN DE LA BARCA? I NEVER KNEW THAT!"

Pablo explained, "Well, technically it's not my name, but I always wanted it to be. It sounds much more regal than just plain old Pablo Gutiérrez. But that's not the point. The point is that if we stick to the plan, you'll be able to have all the paletas you want."

Ugly Cat was so impressed with the plan that he forgot how wrong Pablo had been about little girls being afraid of mice. He could taste the coconut already. He imagined himself lying under a shady tree, with sunglasses, enjoying paleta after paleta after paleta.

"MMMMM . . ." Ugly Cat hadn't realized he had been licking an imaginary treat until Pablo brought him back to reality.

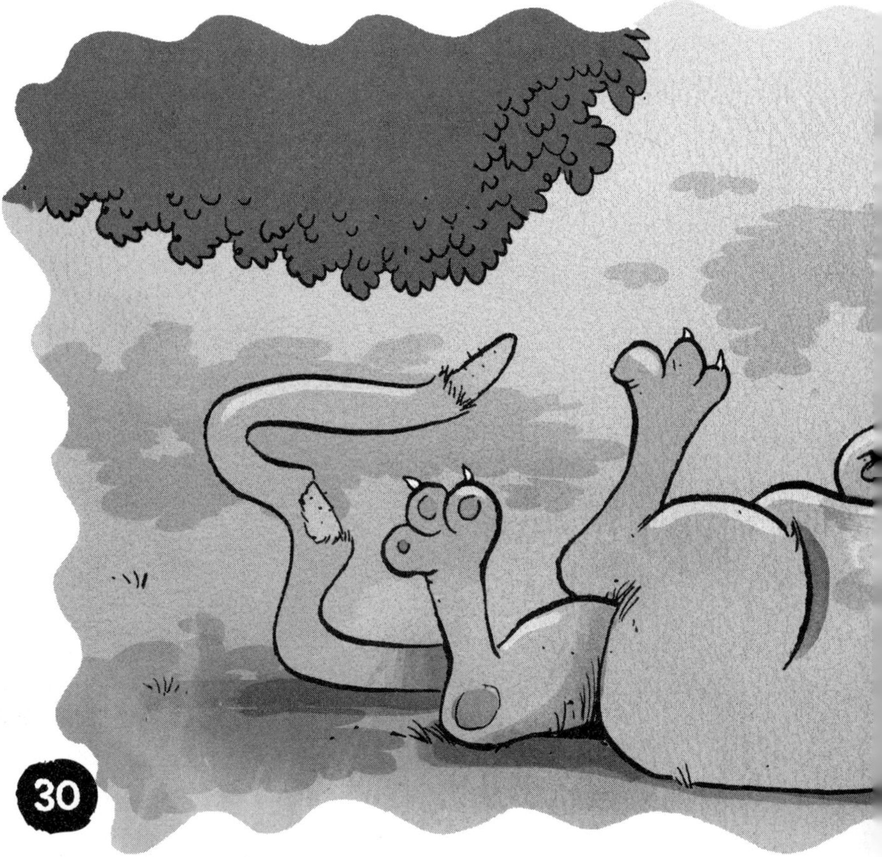

"Ugly! Ugly Cat! Come back to me, man! You don't have a paleta . . . yet! So what do you think of the plan?"

Ugly Cat, still imagining the paleta he'd be eating, eagerly responded, **"PABLO, YOU'RE SO SMART. IT'S A FOOL-PROOF PLAN!"**

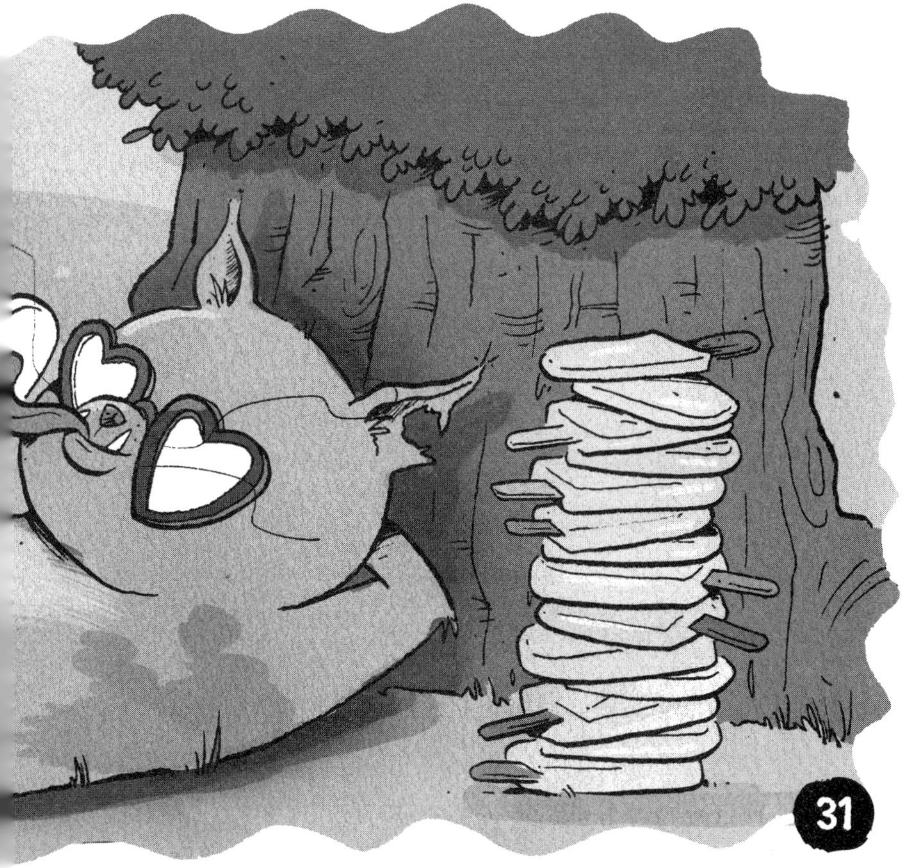

CHAPTER FOUR

The Fool-Proof Plan Gets Fully Foiled

Pablo set the plan in motion. He left Ugly Cat and ran toward the little girl and looked at her. She looked much bigger up close than from far away, but he wasn't going to retreat. No, he had promised Ugly Cat a paleta. He had to make it happen.

Pablo assessed the situation and just knew that creepy-crawling up her leg would have the best scare factor and would positively, absolutely, without a cheddar of a doubt make that wimpy girl drop the prize. He imagined the little girl, feeling his tiny feet and his tail on her leg, realizing that it was a mouse, and

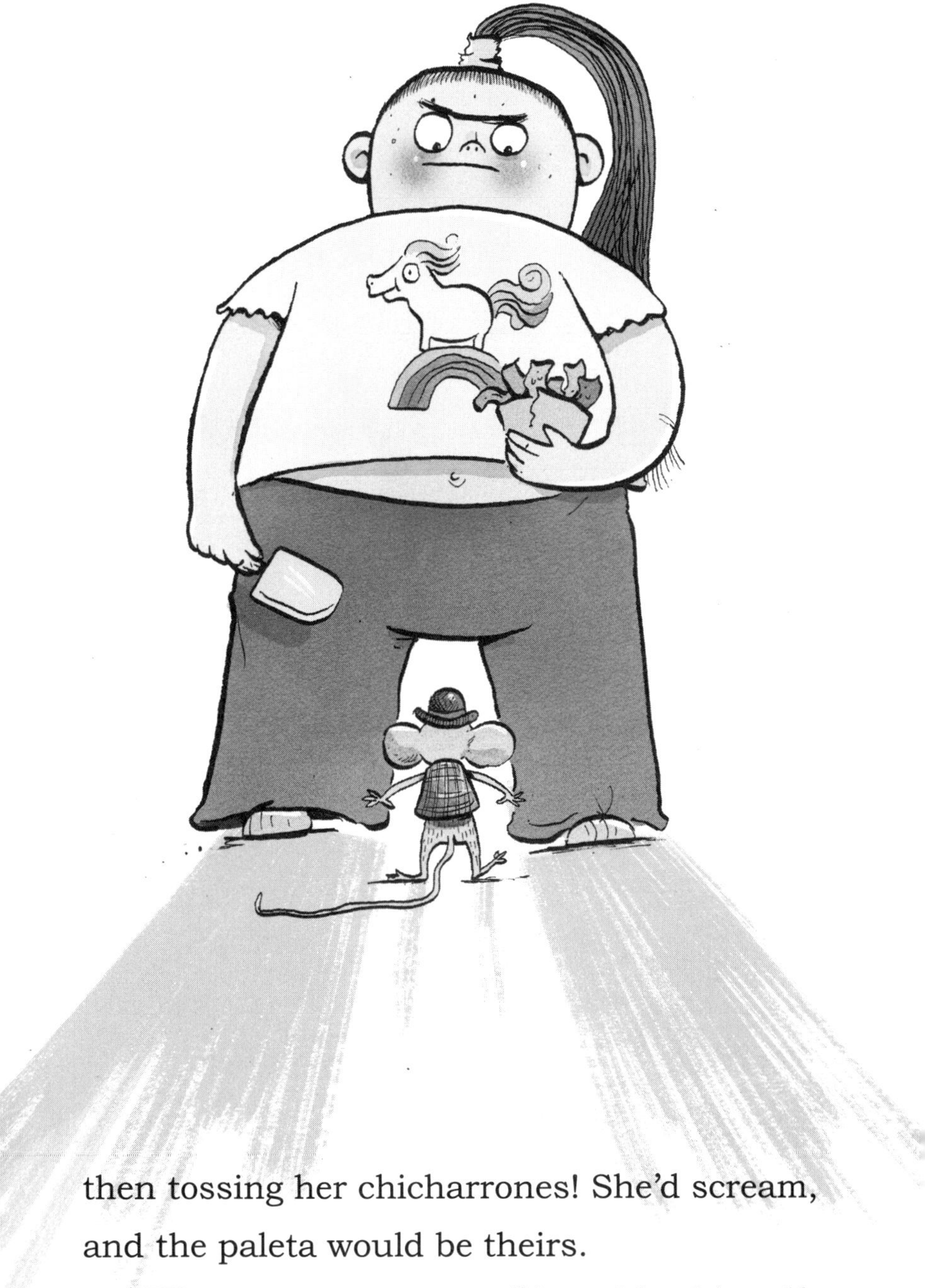

then tossing her chicharrones! She'd scream, and the paleta would be theirs.

"This is too easy," he said to himself.

Pablo jumped on her shoe and began scurrying up her leg. When he reached her knee, he saw her looking down at him. This is it! he thought. She's about to lose it! But instead of losing it like she was supposed to, when the little girl realized what was on her leg, she simply picked up poor, panicked Pablo by his trembling tail and looked at him with loving eyes.

"Oh! What a cute little mouse! I think I'll take him home to feed Rocco," she exclaimed, looking like she'd just caught all the candy out of a piñata.

Ugly Cat had been watching, and suddenly his face had the same look as when Pablo ate all the pepperoni off his pizza. This was definitely not supposed to happen. This was the part of the plan where the little girl was supposed to be screaming! Why was she acting like it was her lucky day that a mouse had crawled up her leg? And why did she call Pablo "**little**"? He hated being called "**little**"! He always referred to himself as "average size" anytime anyone questioned his height. What was wrong with her?!

"WHY DIDN'T YOU LISTEN WHEN I TRIED TO TELL YOU THAT LITTLE GIRLS AREN'T AFRAID OF MICE?" Ugly Cat screamed at Pablo.

But Pablo couldn't hear him. This was way worse than getting kicked out of the park. Actually, getting kicked out of the park seemed like a much better option at the moment. Because Pablo was in serious trouble.

CHAPTER FIVE

Friends Don't Let Friends Become Lunch

Ugly Cat stood frozen. He didn't even notice when Big Mike came up to him.

"What's going on, Ugly? Why do you have that look on your face?"

"PABLO ... PALETA ... ROCCO ..." Ugly Cat tried to explain what happened to Pablo, but he couldn't spit the words out.

"I don't understand what you're saying, Feo." Big Mike realized that Pablo was in trouble. He had no idea what he meant about the paleta or the chicharrones, but he knew who Rocco was. And anything involving him couldn't be good.

"Ugly! Ugly Cat! Snap out of it!" The cat still wasn't responding, so Big Mike did the only thing he thought would bring him back—he licked Ugly Cat's face.

"SPLECH . . . WHAT THE . . . BiG MiKE? WHAT ARE YOU DOiNG HERE? I'VE NEVER BEEN SO HAPPY TO SEE A DOG iN MY LiFE!"

Big Mike shook his head. "I've been here for a while, but you were somewhere else. Anyway, I'm here because I was still feeling sad and Mindy decided to take me for a walk at the park. She's over there by the frozen bananas." Big Mike nodded at his owner. "I wasn't going to talk to you ever again, but then I saw what was happening with Pablo and—"

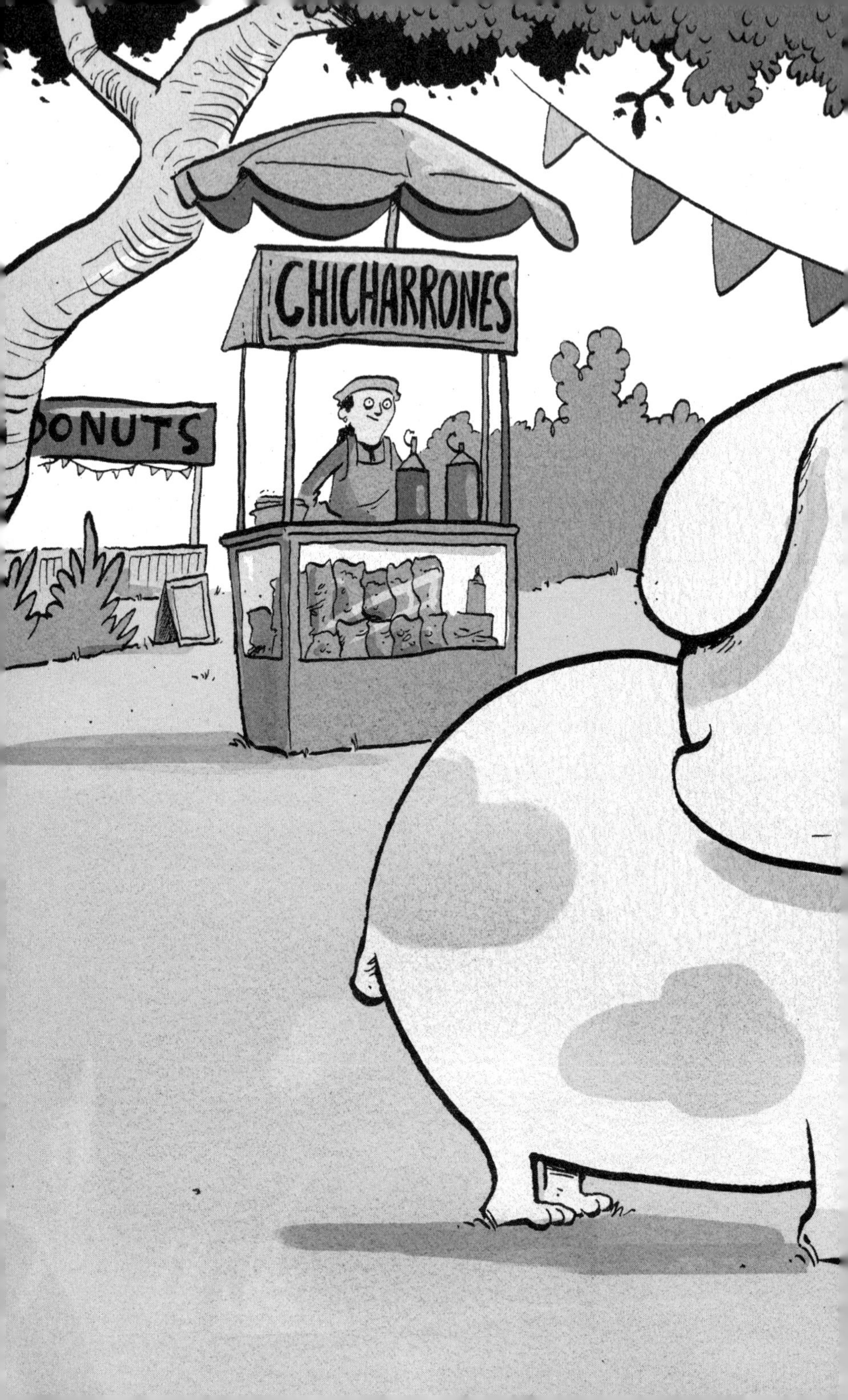
CHICHARRONES
DONUTS

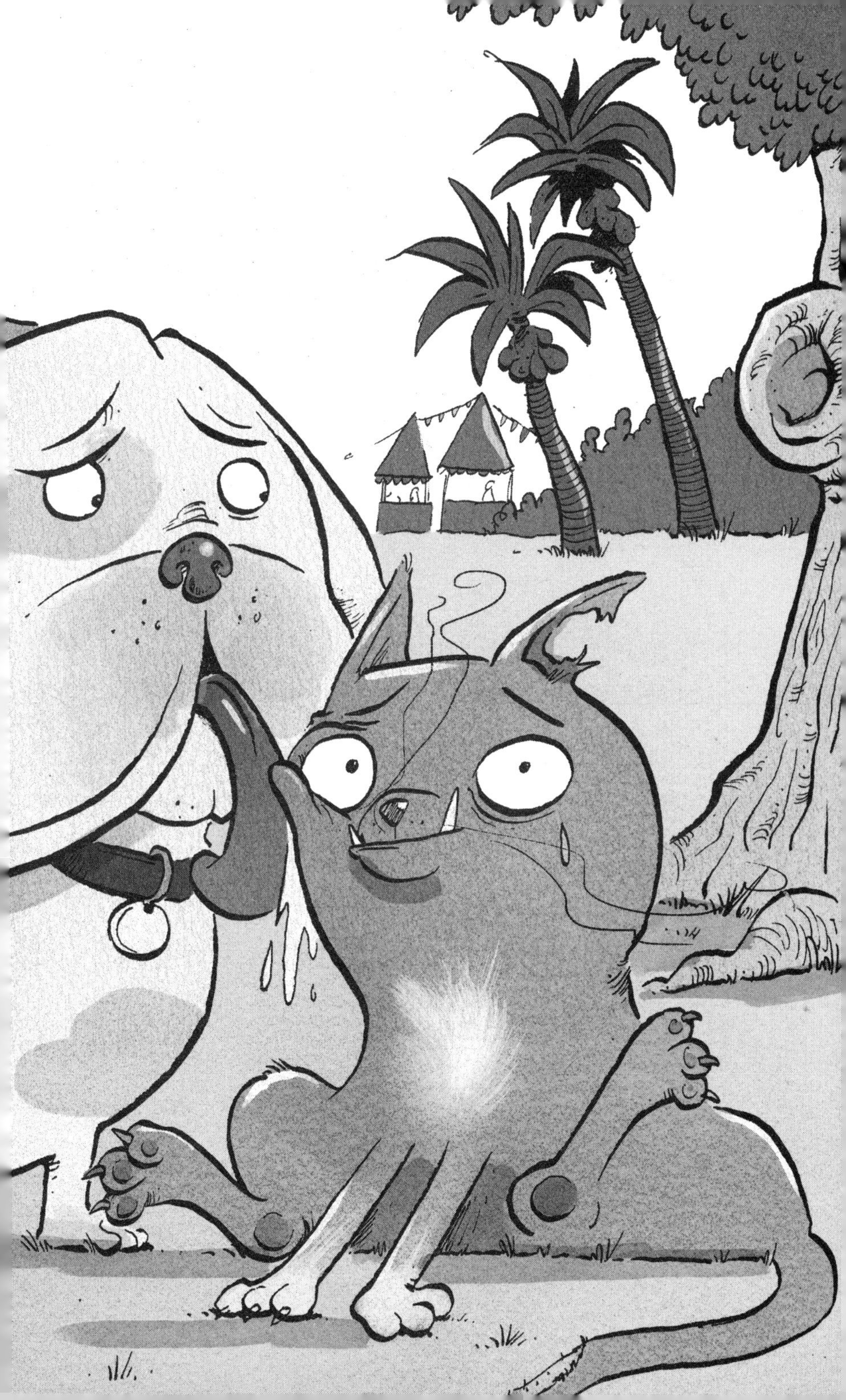

All the things that Ugly Cat didn't know how to say about the rodeo incident came rushing out of him. "I KNOW WE HAVE TO HELP PABLO, BUT FIRST I HAVE TO TELL YOU THAT I'M SO SORRY ABOUT BEING SUCH A HORRIBLE FRIEND YESTERDAY, MAN. WE SHOULD HAVE STOPPED WHEN YOU SAID STOP. WE GOT CARRIED AWAY. IF THERE IS FORGIVENESS IN YOUR BIG, BEAUTIFUL CORAZÓN, CAN THAT FORGIVENESS PLEASE COME QUICKLY AND ALSO APPLY TO PABLO?

HE'S IN A VERY PRECARIOUS SITUATION. THAT GIRL JUST SAID SHE WAS GOING TO FEED HIM TO SOMEONE NAMED ROCCO."

Big Mike yelped. "Rocco is bad news."

"YOU KNOW WHO THAT IS? YOU KNOW EVERYBODY. REMEMBER THAT ONE TIME WE SNUCK INTO THE POUND AND YOU KNEW ALMOST ALL THE DOGS THERE? I WAS LIKE, 'OH MY GATO, BIG MIKE, YOU'RE SUCH A POPULAR PUP.' AND YOU WERE LIKE, 'NAW, BUT MINDY DOES GET ME TO THE DOG PARK AND ALL THESE DUDES HAVE—'"

Big Mike interrupted the rambling feline. "Ugly Cat! Come on, focus! Yes, I know a lot of dogs. But Rocco is definitely not a dog. You know who he is, too, don't you remember?"

Suddenly, Ugly Cat remembered where he'd heard the name. A few weeks before, Ugly Cat, Pablo, and Big Mike had been walking through the neighborhood, when they heard a little girl three houses down, throwing a horrible tantrum.

"YOU'RE SO UNFAIR! CAN'T YOU SEE THAT I NEED A SNAKE? I WANT A BOA TO LOVE AND HOLD AND I'LL CALL HIM ROCCO AND WE'LL BE BEST FRIENDS!" She was really into it, too: fake sobbing, feet stomping, and—the coup de grace—throwing herself on the floor. They had all laughed at how she had thrown herself on the ground and started wiggling around. She had looked so ridiculous, the three had been sure that she wouldn't get the snake. But her parents weren't that kind of parents. Ugly Cat, Pablo, and Mike found this out when they saw the little girl a few days later taking her boa out for a walk and talking baby talk to it.

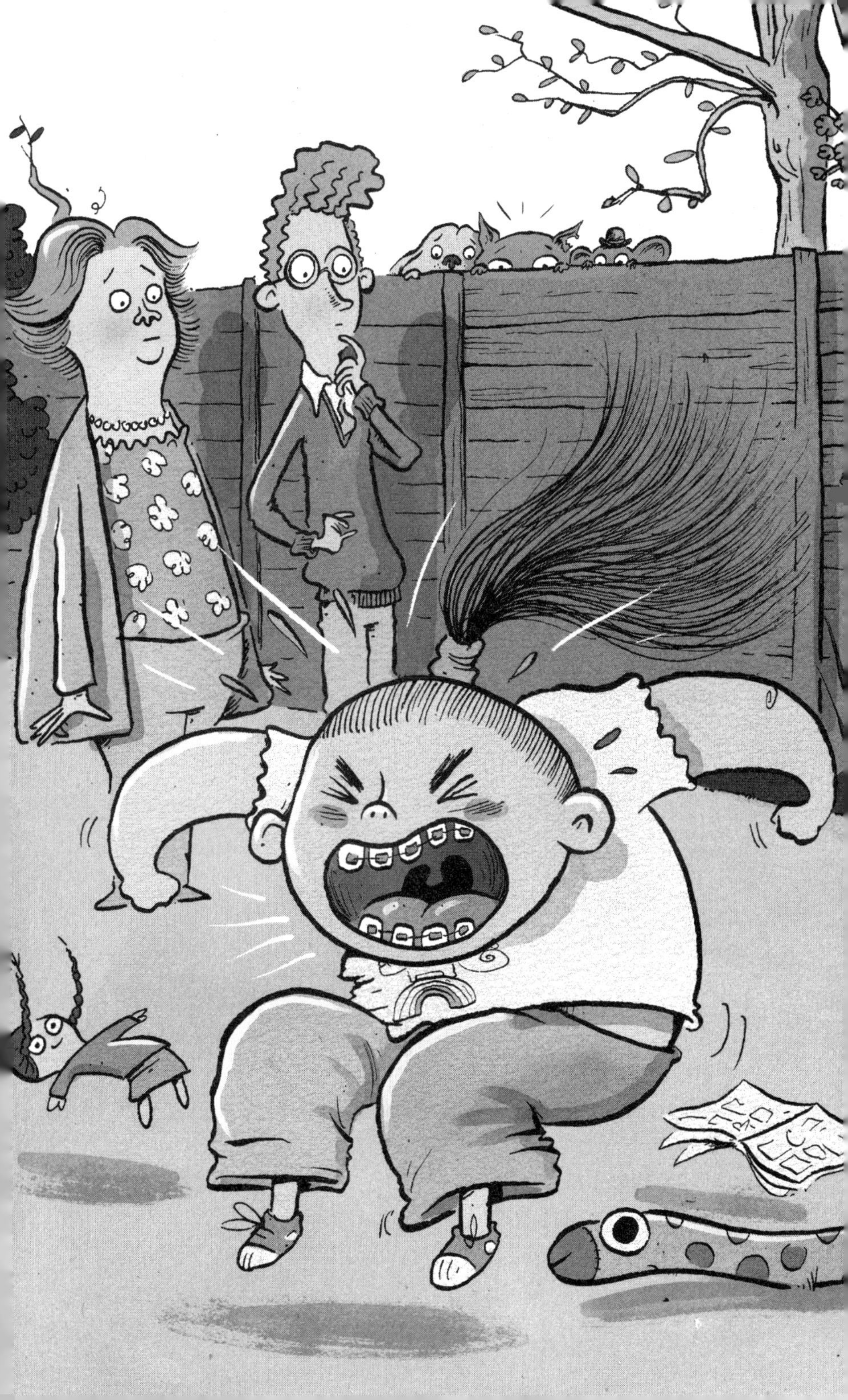

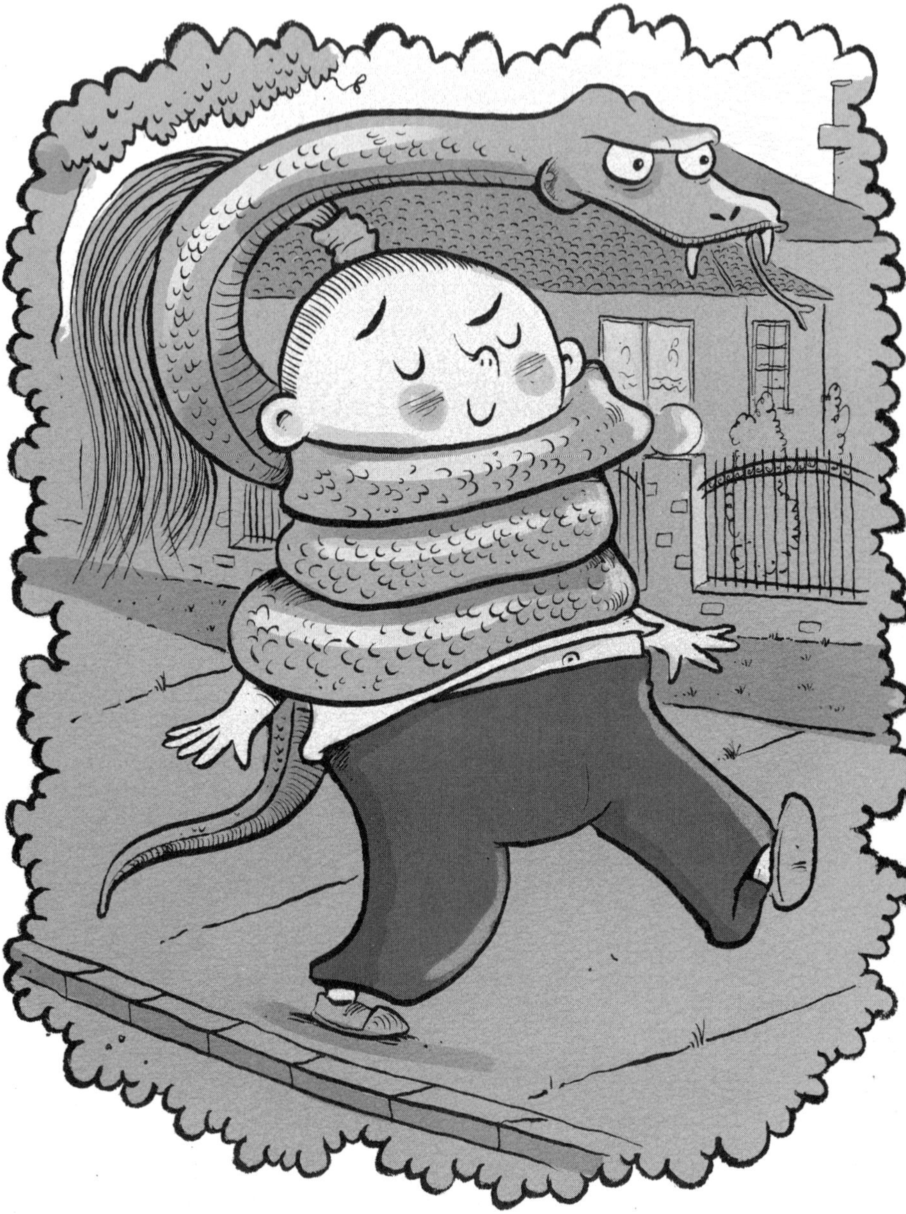

"HOW COULD I FORGET? ROCCO IS THE BIGGEST CONSTRICTOR I HAVE EVER SEEN!" Ugly Cat said.

"That's right, and if we don't hurry up, Pablo is gonna be a snake snack for sure!" exclaimed Big Mike.

"Help! Ayúdenme!" Pablo was still being held near the little girl's face and his voice was faint, but his friends heard him, and that was all that mattered.

Big Mike and Ugly Cat nodded at each other and leapt into Operation Make Sure Pablo Doesn't Become Rocco's Lunch.

The English bulldog charged at the little girl with all the fierceness he had, barking and growling and pretending to nip at her ankles. He couldn't bring himself to ever really bite anyone (that was just gross).

"What the—get away, you crazy dog!" The little girl tried kicking him, but Big Mike kept barking and growling.

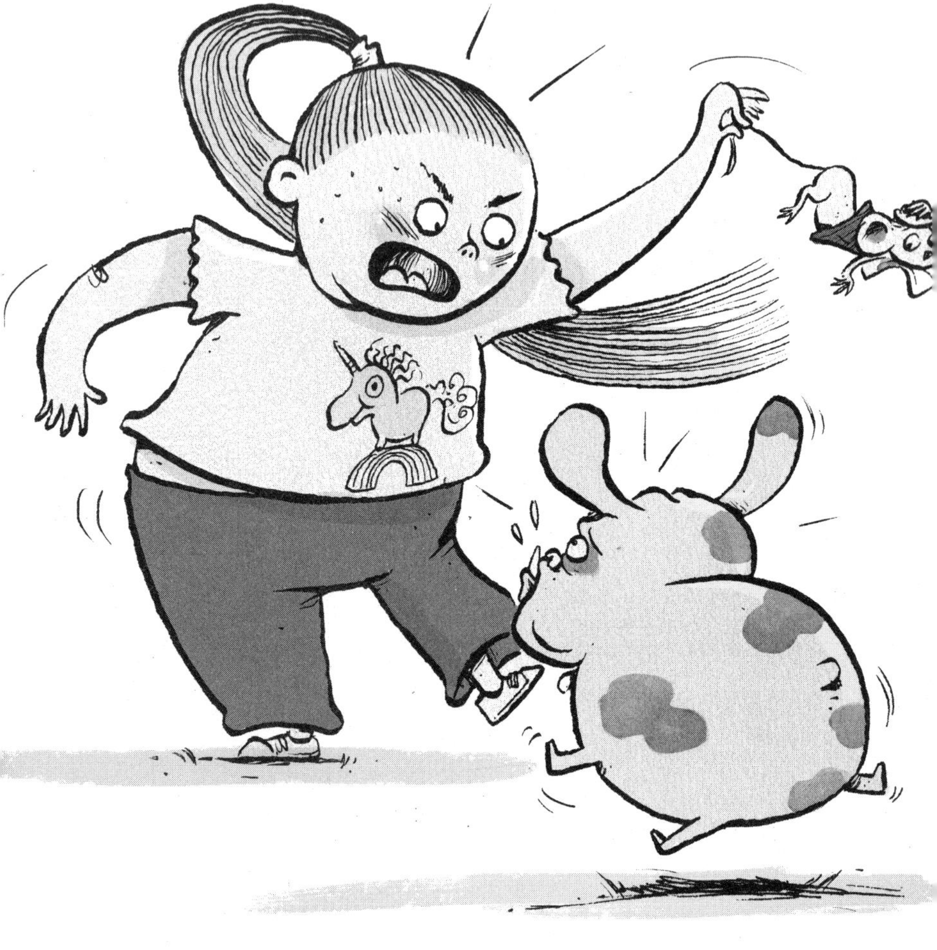

Mindy heard all the ruckus and ran over, three chocolate-covered bananas in hand.

"I am so very sorry!" she said, pulling her dog away. **"Big Mike! What's wrong with you! Bad dog! Very bad dog!"**

Big Mike turned around and saluted Ugly Cat, shouting, "His fate is in your hands now, comrade!"

Ugly Cat nodded and extended his claws. It was now or never see his best friend again.

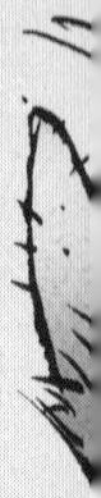

CHAPTER SIX

Safety First, but Paletas Shortly After

Faster than the speed of a snail and quicker than a tick in a bath, Ugly Cat jumped up onto the paleta cart and let out a bloodcurdling battle cry. He hissed and bared his teeth like he was a cat possessed.

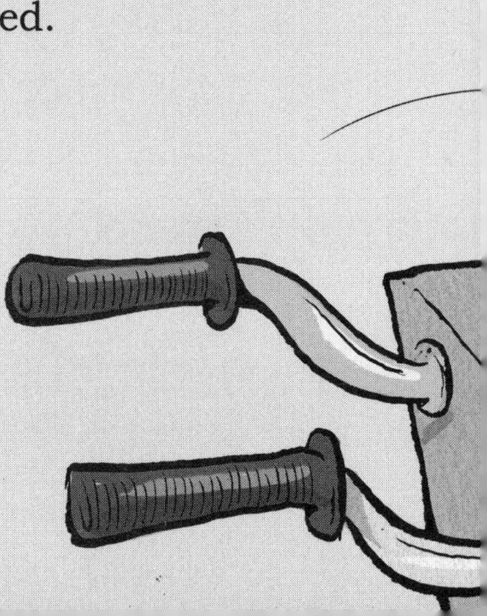

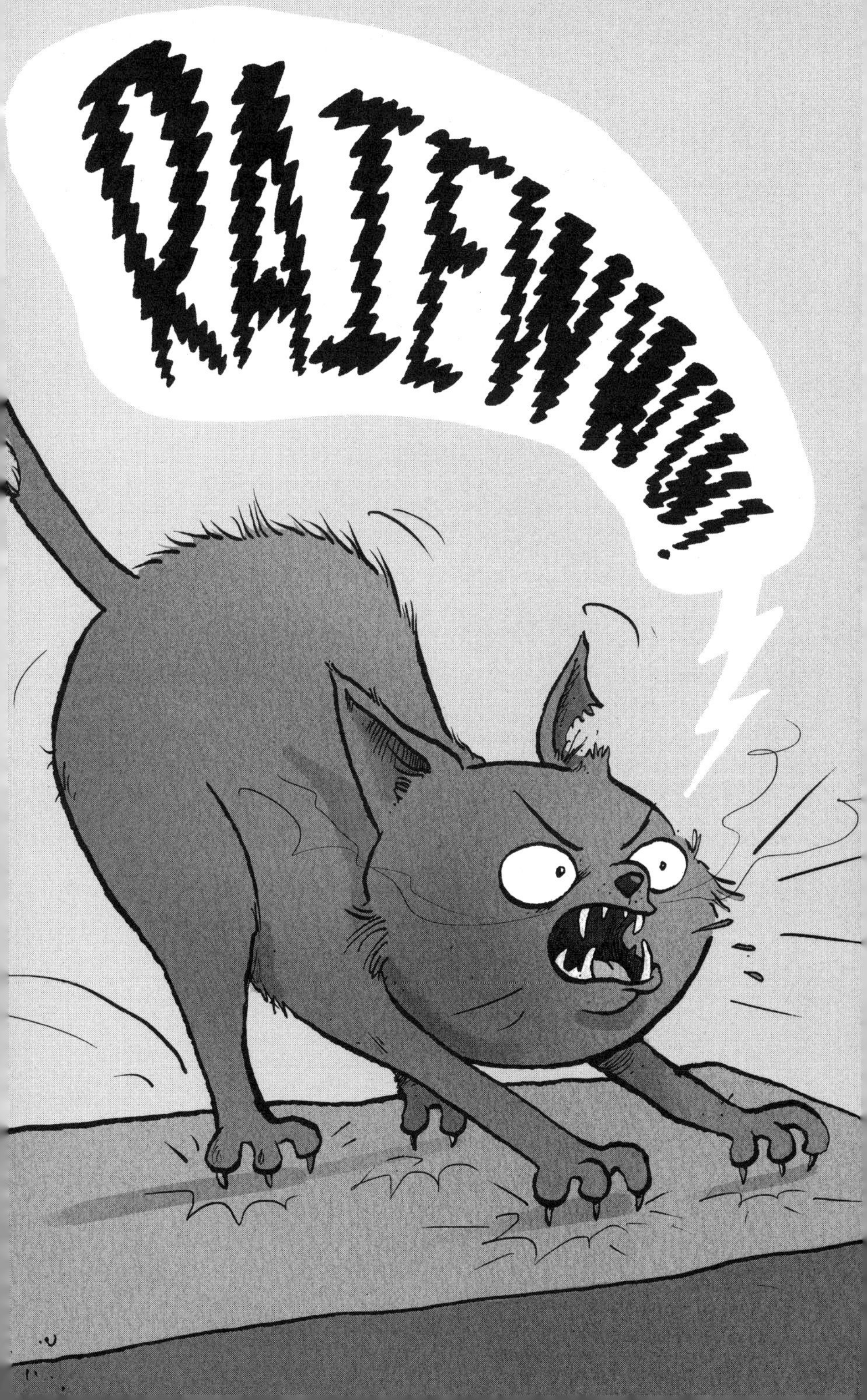
RAIEWWW!

The poor paletero didn't know whether to leave his cart or save his delicious creations. He decided to stay and fight, but when Ugly Cat accidentally scratched his pinkie, he booked it, yelling over his shoulder to his paletas.

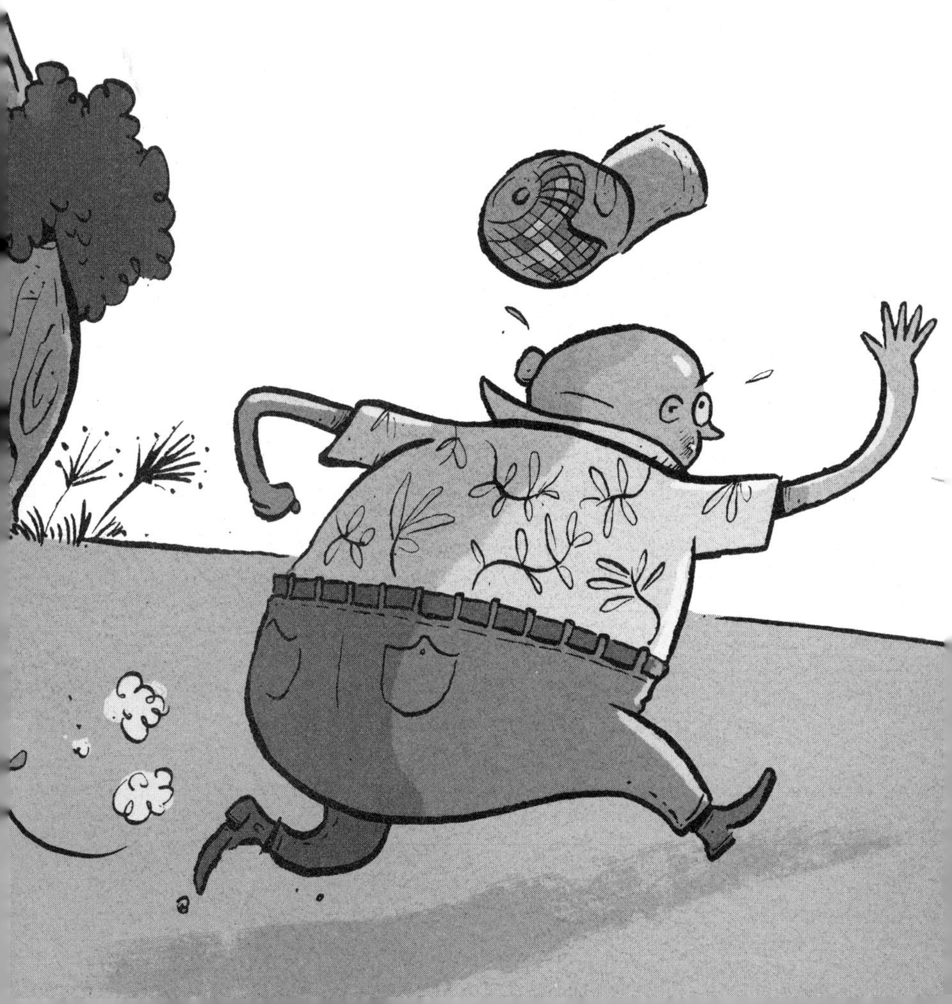

Ugly Cat felt bad about accidentally scratching the paletero—that hadn't been part of the plan. OH NO! I HOPE HE'S OKAY! I HOPE HE'LL STILL BE ABLE TO MAKE PALETAS! he thought.

Then Ugly turned toward the little girl and tried to grab Pablo with his mouth. This wasn't really part of the plan, either, but he had to improvise. The little girl would think that he'd eaten the mouse, and Ugly Cat would let him go as soon as they got to a safe place. All Pablo would need would be a soapy scrub, and he'd be as good as new.

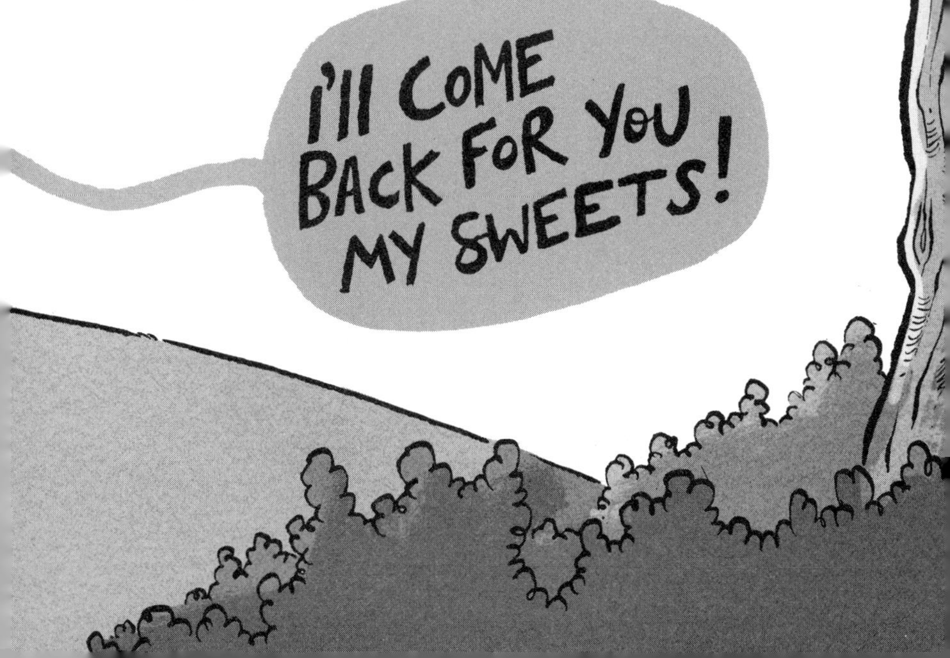
I'LL COME BACK FOR YOU MY SWEETS!

But when Ugly Cat opened his mouth to take Pablo to safety, Pablo squirmed and the little girl accidentally dropped the poor mouse. Ugly Cat's face was so spine-chillingly convincing that Pablo believed Ugly had forgotten the cross-his-heart-and-hope-to-die-stick-a-needle-in-his-eye promise that he made long ago when they first met (the I-promise-never-to-eat-you promise). He was sure he'd soon be saying "good mornin'" to the inside of Ugly Cat's stomach and "good-bye" to pepper jack cheese and bacon wraps forever.

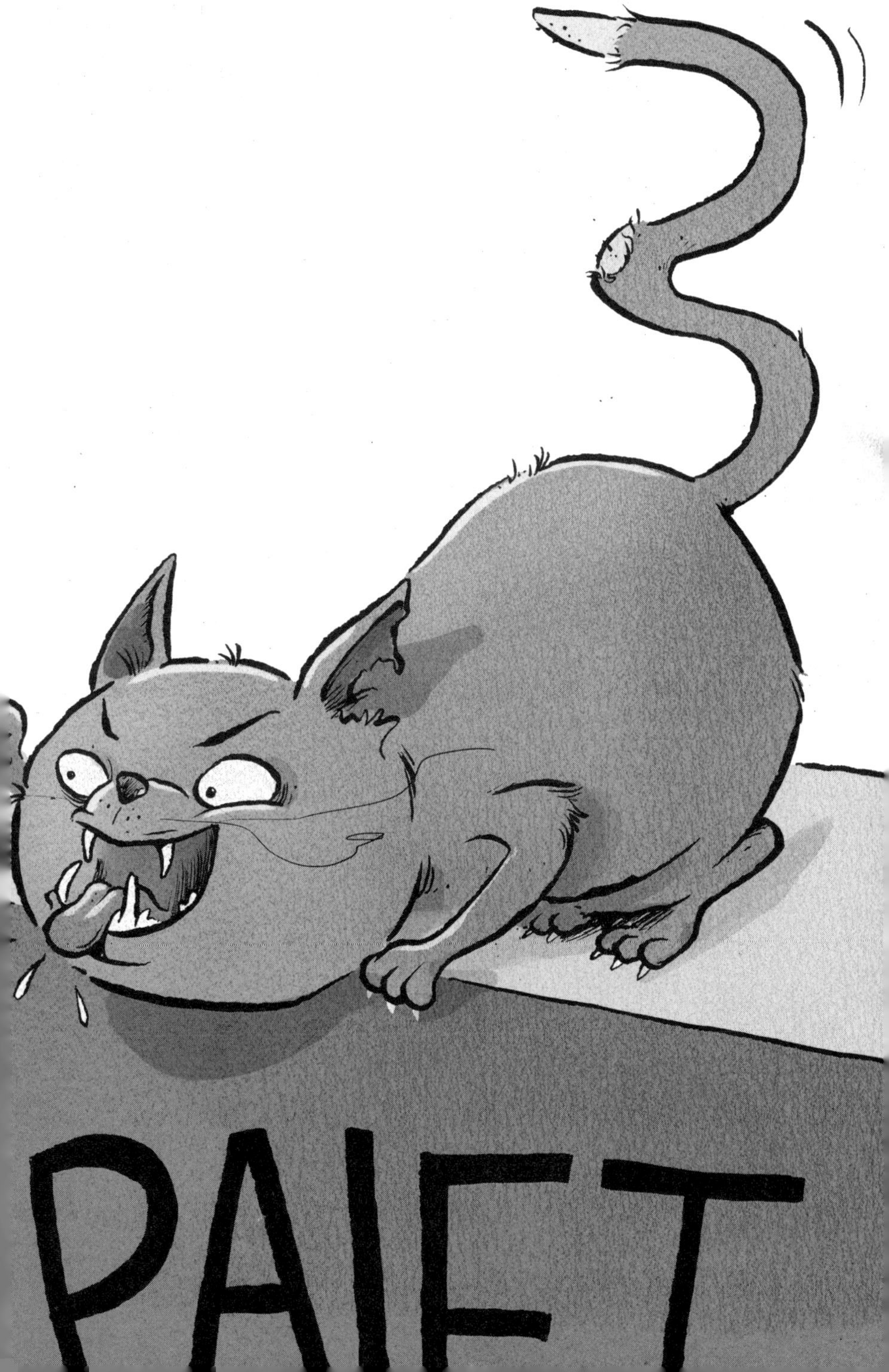
PAIFT

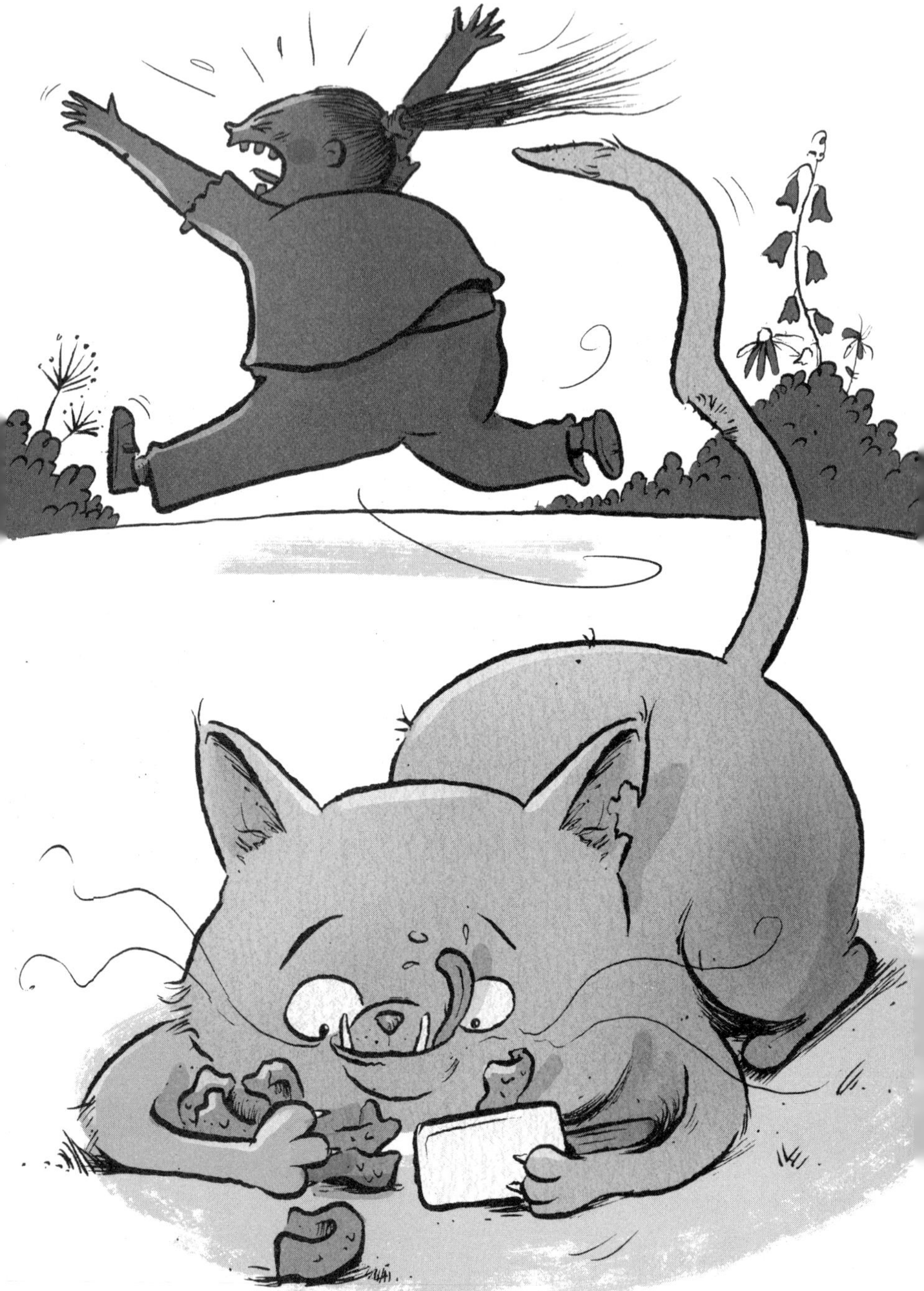

Pablo didn't want to die as someone's lunch. He had his dignity and had to act fast. As soon as his feet hit the ground, he zipped out of there. The little girl screamed (clearly this girl loved screaming), **"THESE ANIMALS HAVE LOST THEIR FUR-BRAINED MINDS!"** She threw her coconut paleta and her bag of chicharrones on the ground, exasperated, and ran off to throw a fit.

Now, if there was anything that could shift Ugly Cat's concentration from a rescue mission to a food mission, it was a paleta, and so the cat didn't notice that his best friend had run off.

"PALETAAAAA!" Ugly Cat screamed as he jumped down from the white cart and grabbed the frosty treat. And then he snatched up the chicharrones, too, because it would be a waste if he didn't.

Ugly Cat turned to share his bounty with Pablo, forgetting all about what had just happened, he was so overcome with joy. **"PABLO! PABLO! PABLO! LOOK! LOOK! IT'S OUR LUCKY DAY! WE GOT A TWO-FOR-ONE DEAL WITH THIS GIRL!"**

But Pablo, still fearing that Ugly Cat was going to eat him, had rocketed out of the festival before he became cat chow. So, naturally, like any good friend would do, Ugly Cat ran after him.

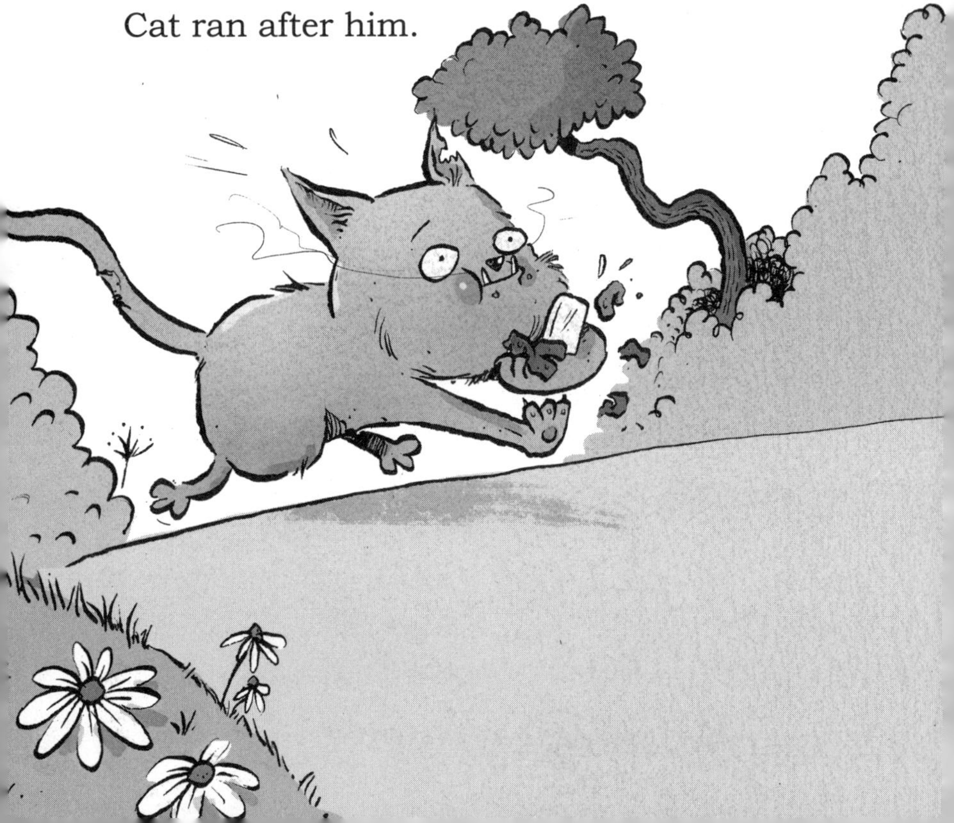

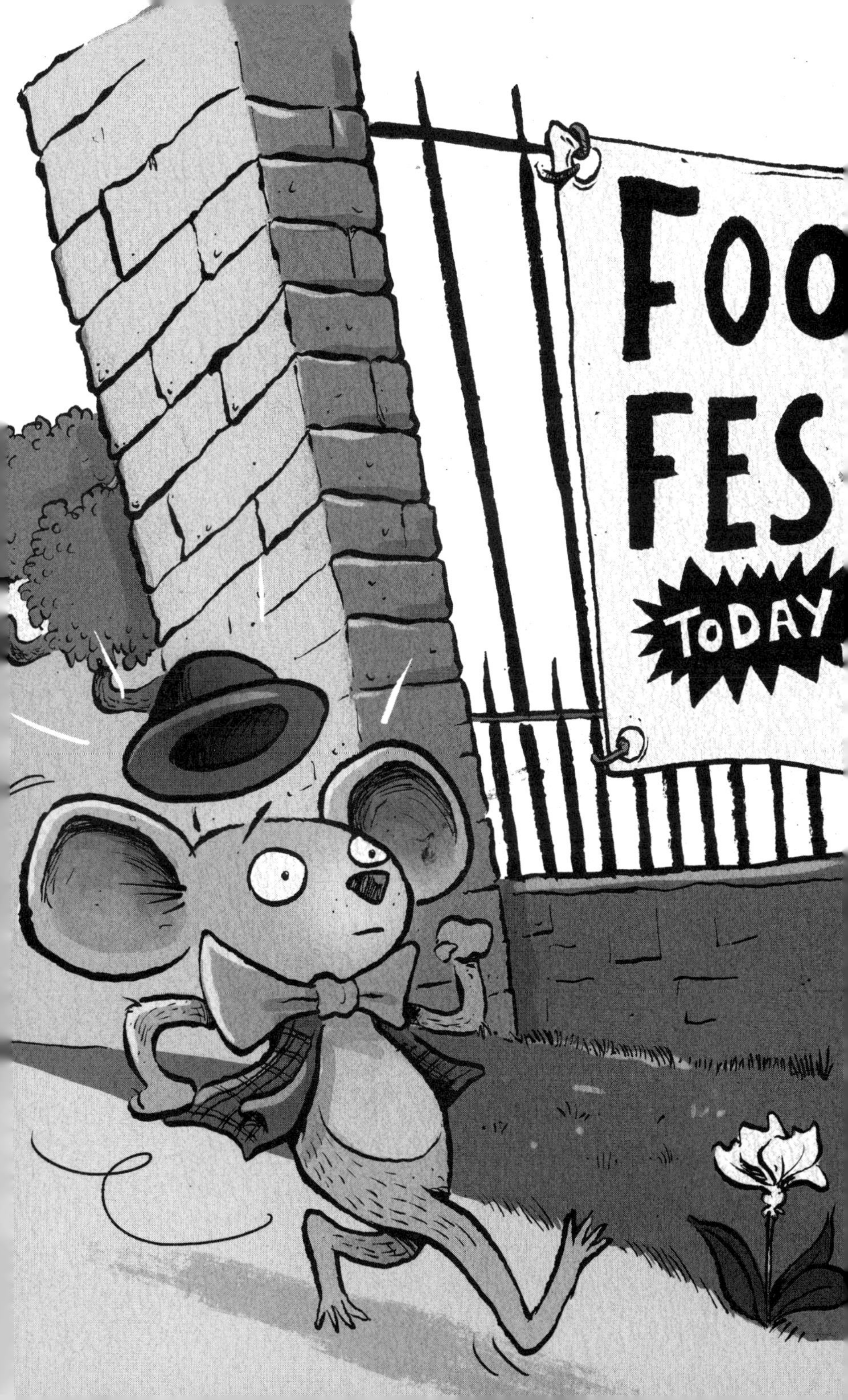
FOO
FES
TODAY

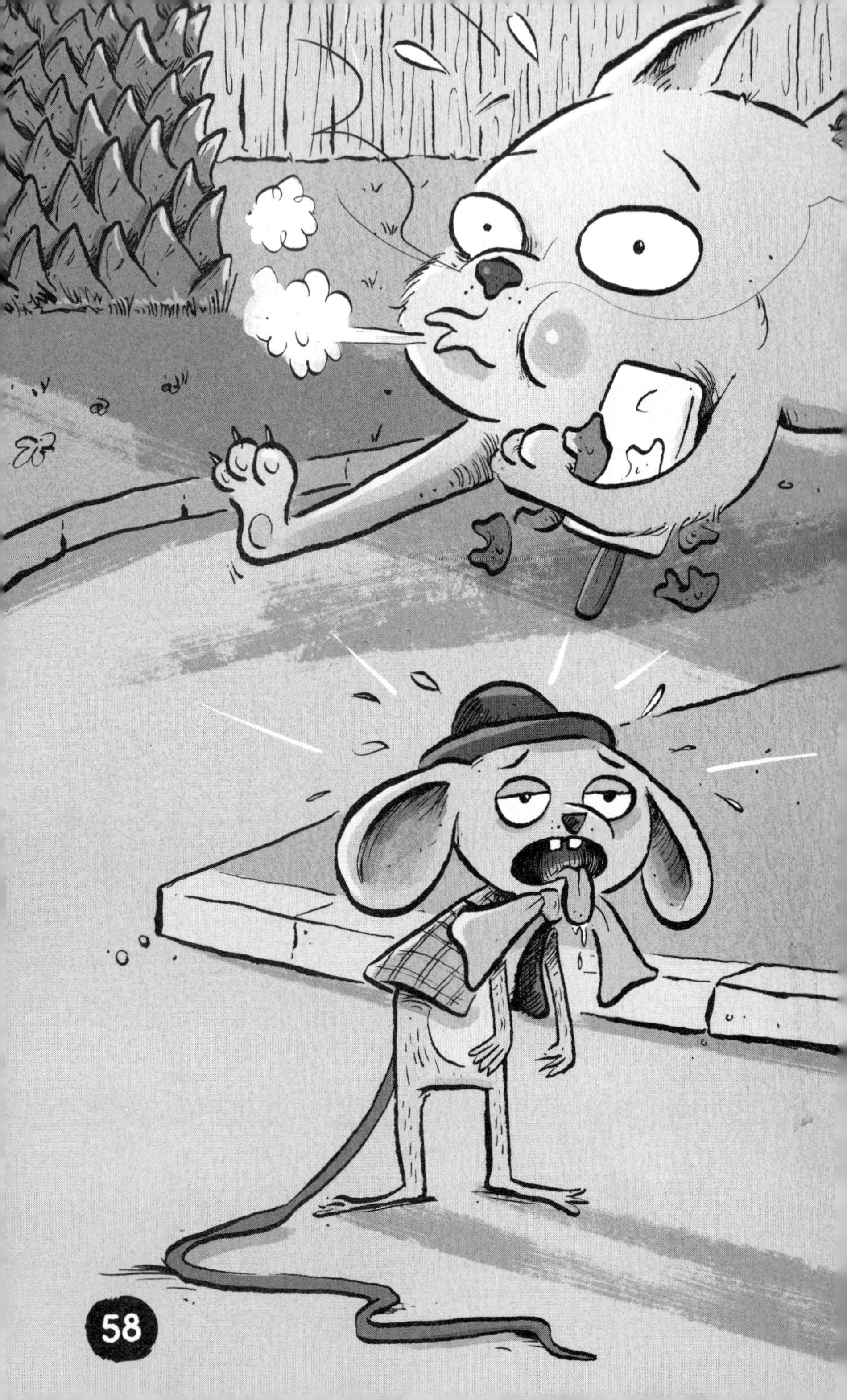

CHAPTER SEVEN

A Little Misunderstanding

When Ugly Cat finally caught up with Pablo, the big cat was really, really tired. **"PA"**—gasp—**"BLO"**—gasp—**"PA"**—gasp—**"BLO"**—gasp—**"STOP. STOOOOOP."** He could barely breathe. **I REALLY NEED TO STOP EATING SO MANY PALETAS AND CHICHARRONES**, Ugly Cat thought as he stopped and shoved another chicharrón in his mouth and took another sloppy lick of the paleta, which was beginning to melt. He was getting it all over himself.

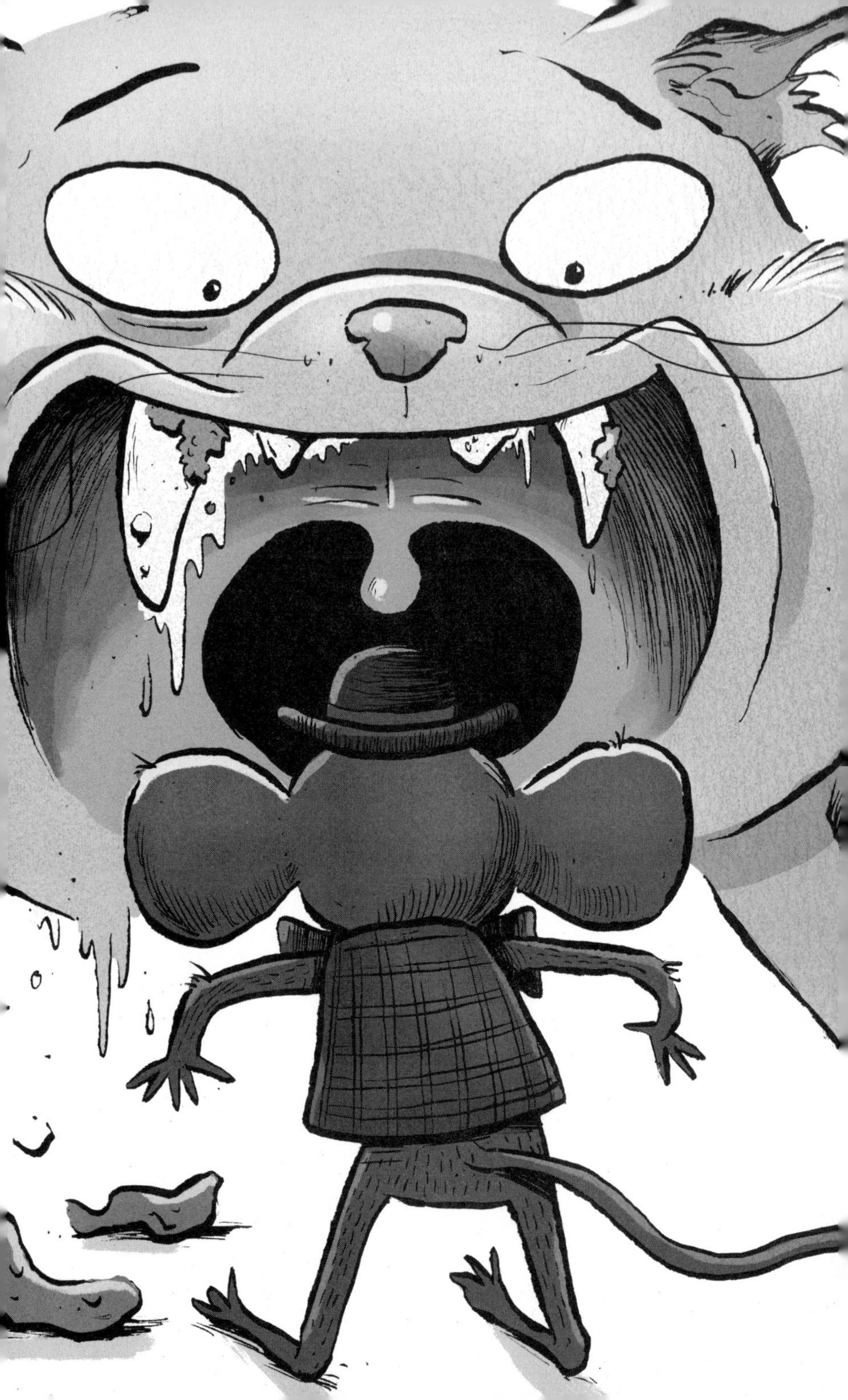

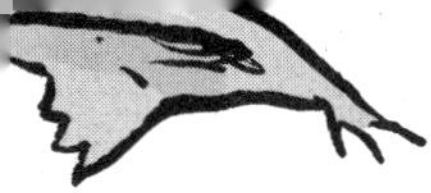

Pablo stopped running. His little legs couldn't move another inch. His body ached all over, and his hat was dripping with sweat. Pablo sat down. Ugly Cat stood over him. The cat's mouth was wide open, full of chewed-up snacks. His whiskers were covered in coconut cream, and he cried, **"PABLOOO!"** spitting food everywhere.

Pablo looked up at the cat in terrified disbelief. Would his best friend really chase him down to make him the third and most delicious course on his lunch menu?

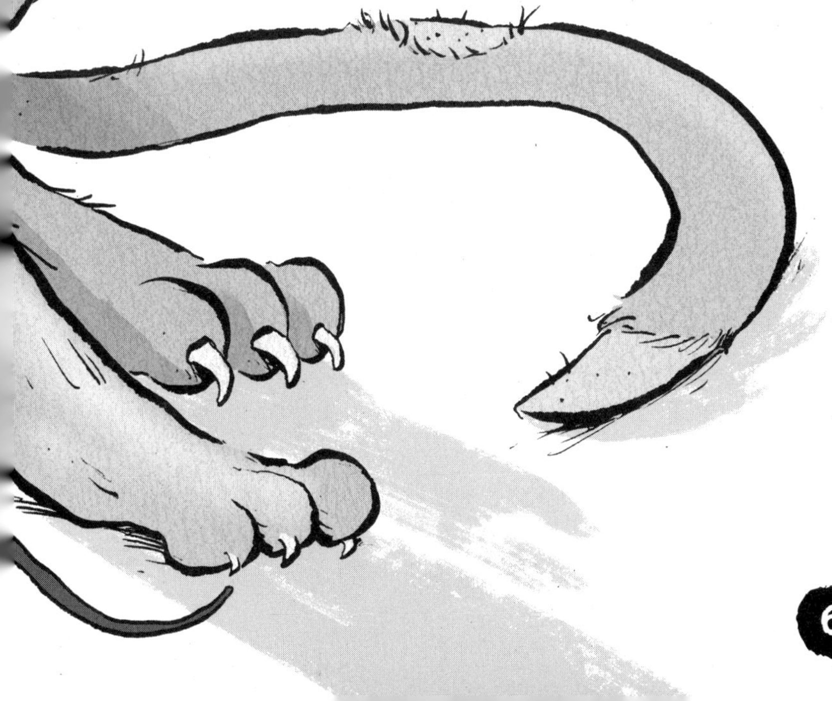

"Ugly Cat! Why? Why? I thought we were amigos hasta el final? It hurts. Aquí me duele, right here," he cried, pounding on his small gray chest.

"WAIT. WHAT? PABLO, I WAS JUST TR—" Ugly Cat tried to clarify things, but Pablo wasn't having it.

Pablo stood up. He stared at Ugly Cat, fixed his sweaty hat, and puffed out his chest. "No, no, no, gatito. I will not cry anymore, Mr. Let's-Be-Best-Friends-Forever! Mr. Cross-My-Heart-and-Hope-to-Die-Stick-a-Needle-in-My-Eye that he would never ever eat Pablo! No! You are a liar and a disgrace to your species. You backstabbing filthy feline! You treacherous tabby! You murderous mouse muncher!"

"QUÉ LA ENCHILADA! PABLO, LOOK, LET'S—" But Ugly Cat didn't have a chance to finish.

Pablo had found a weapon with which to make his last stand: a discarded toothpick. He grabbed it and leapt dramatically at Ugly Cat's leg, yelling:

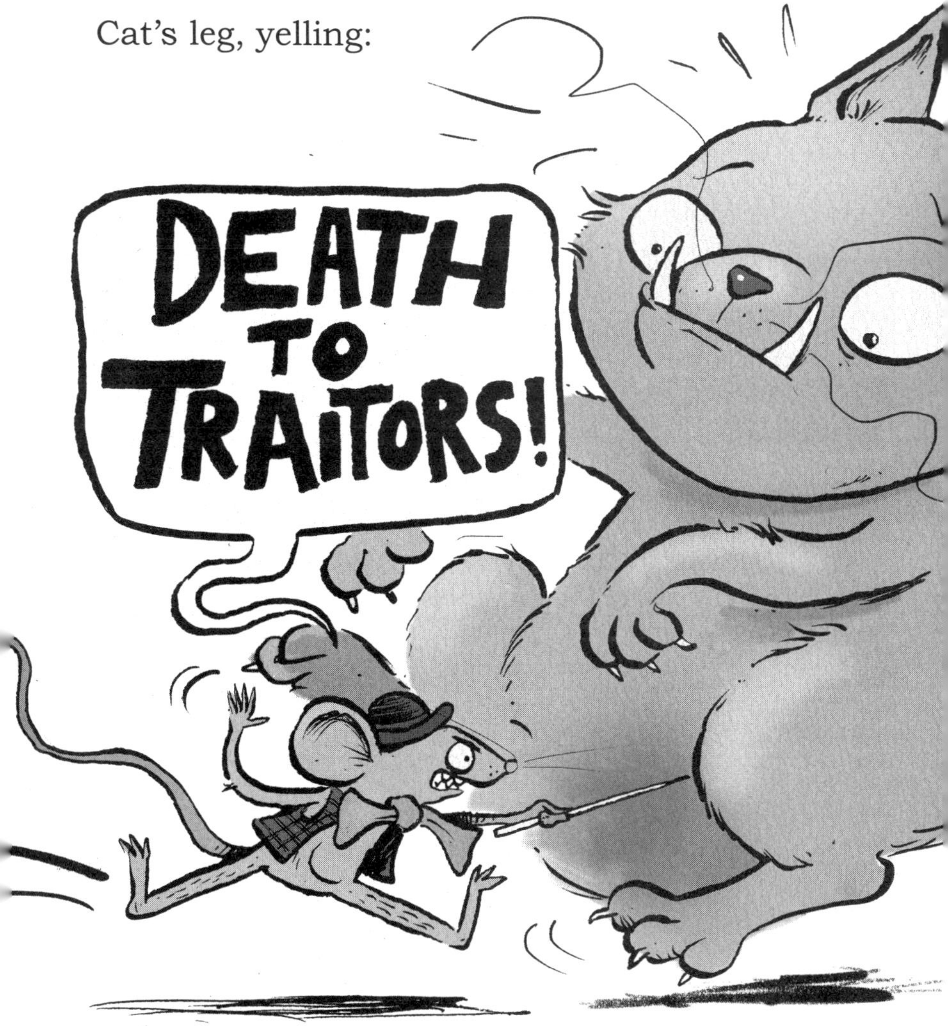
DEATH TO TRAITORS!

It would have been a spectacular attempt, but Pablo misjudged the length of the jump and landed two inches too short, face-first at Ugly Cat's paws.

Ugly Cat was so confused by Pablo's actions. **"WHAT ARE YOU TALKING ABOUT?"** he said. However, since his mouth was full of crunchy chicharrón goodness, Pablo heard it as **"WALK INTO MY MOUTH,"** and that made Pablo angrier.

"Hmph. Lazy, too, huh? Well, what could I expect from a conniving cat like you? Fine. I'll walk into your mouth. Only because my legs are tired from running so much and I can't run anymore. Let it be known that Pablo Gutiérrez Calderón de la Barca faced his finale without fear." Then Pablo begged, "But please, Ugly, just swallow me whole. I can't stand the thought of my little body being bitten in half." He sniffled as he took off his plaid vest, folded it neatly on the ground, then gave his hat a quick kiss and placed it on top of the vest.

He looked up at Ugly Cat and through tears said, "So you won't choke, old friend."

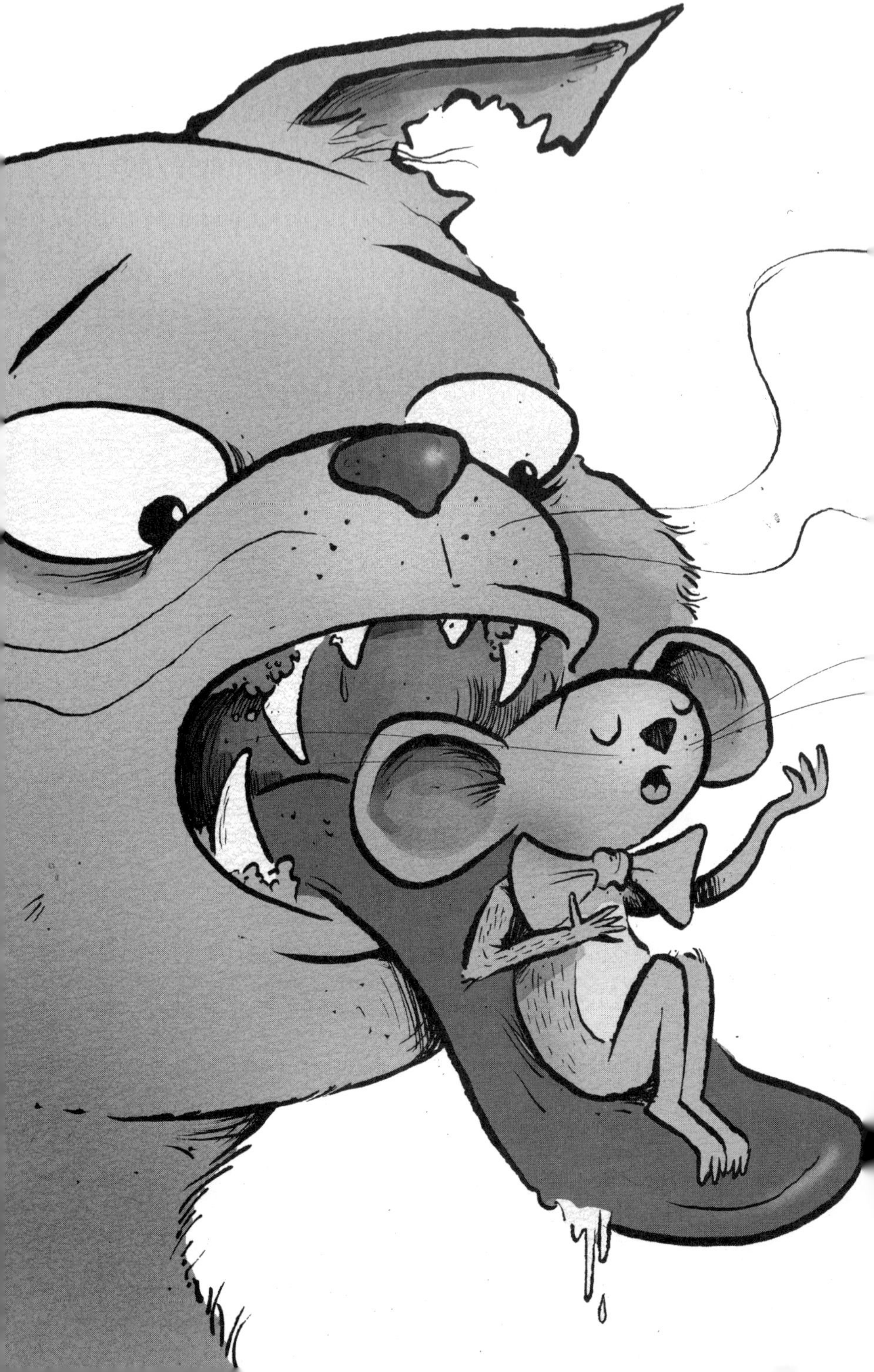

Pablo climbed up Ugly Cat's back, over his ears, and down his nose, directly into his stinky, chicharrón-filled mouth.

Ugly Cat stood there with his mouth wide open. The mouse crawled right on in and sat smack down in the middle of the cat's tongue. "Good-bye, sweet world! How I loved living you, life! Mama! Mama, I'm comin' home! Your sweet Pablito, the smallest of your ratoncitos, is comin' to see you!"

Then he poked his head out and looked up at Ugly Cat. "I will never forget the good times, Ugly, even if I am just another tasty and exceptionally tender treat! Ya listo, I am ready to go now." He sat back down on Ugly Cat's tongue, took a deep breath, and waited for the cat to swallow.

And then, suddenly the cat did.

CHAPTER EIGHT

The Cat Who Went Splat

Ugly Cat accidentally started to swallow Pablo. His natural cat reflexes, the ones he thought he'd given up, the mouse-eating ones, took over! As soon as the cat closed his mouth, Pablo turned his tender little body around and started scratching his way free. He wasn't as ready to say good-bye to the sweet, sweet world as he had thought.

"I changed my mind! I changed my mind! I want to live! I'm not ready for mouse heaven! Ha-ha-ha! I was just

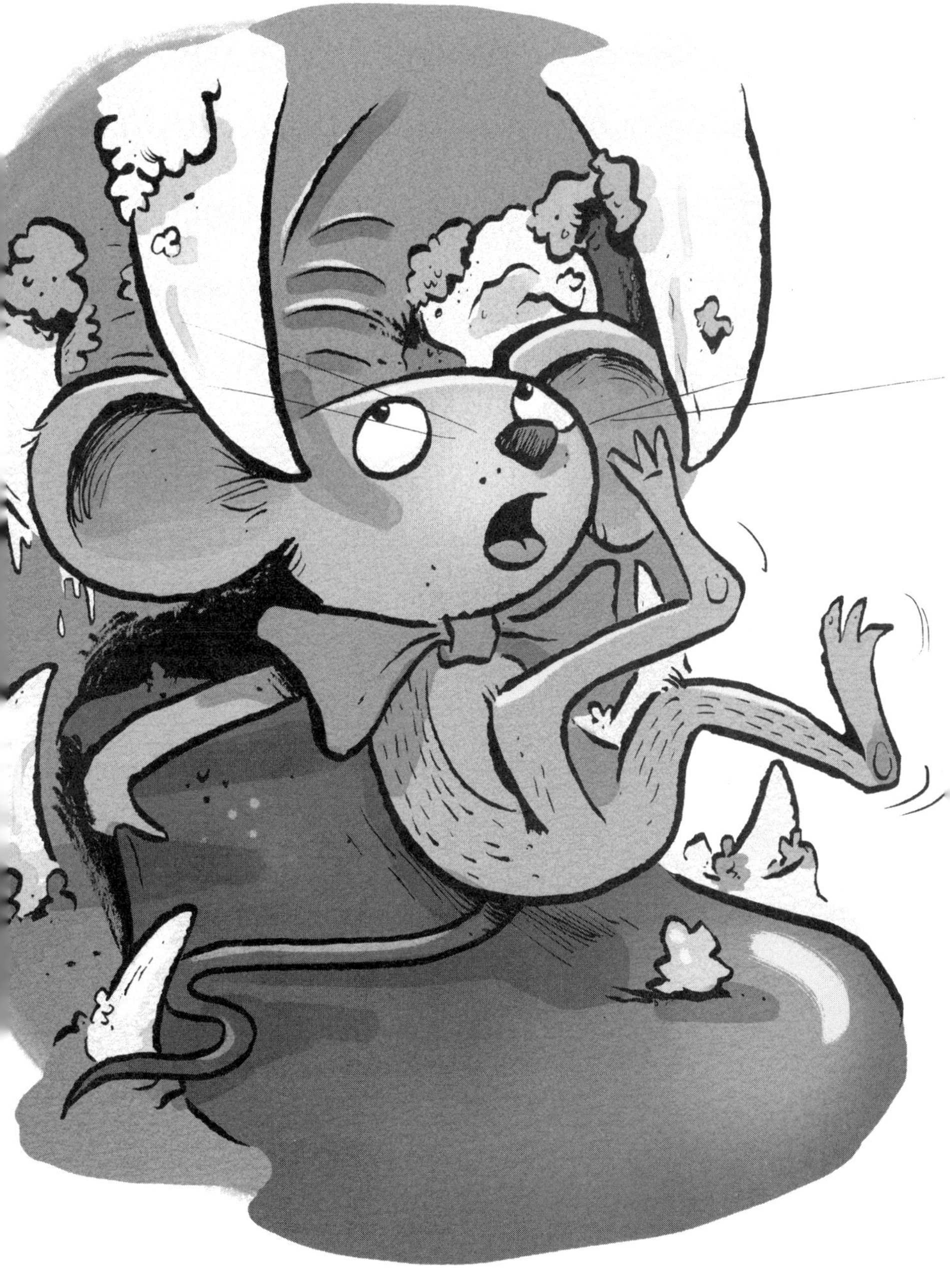

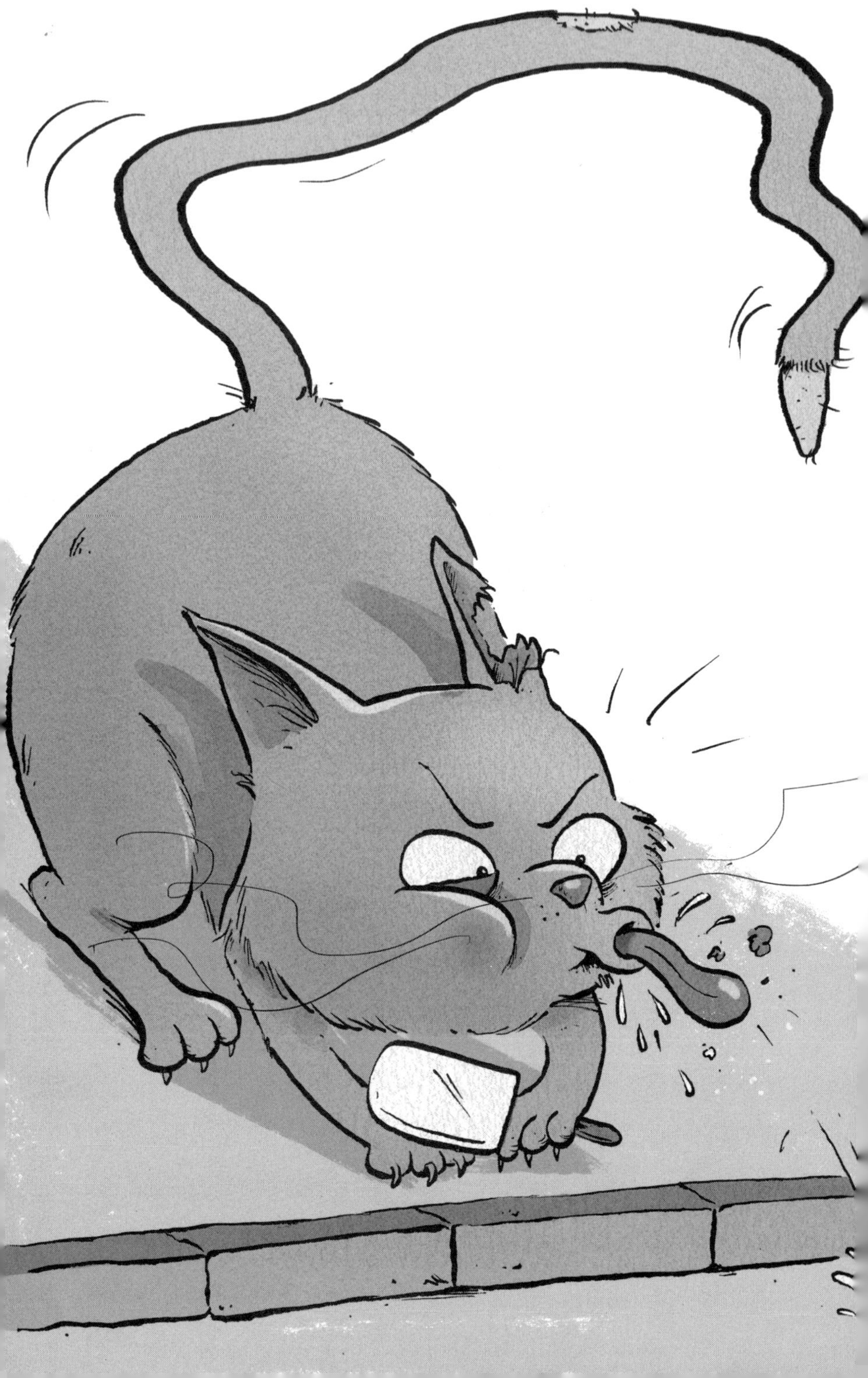

joking! See? Qué chistoso! Ha! Ha! Ugly! Ugly! Open up! Have some pity on your poor pal Pablito!" Pablo hung on to Ugly Cat's tongue with his little claws.

Ugly spit him out.

"WHAT WERE YOU DOING, PABLO?! EWWW! I DON'T EAT MICE ANYMORE! YOU KNOW THAT. THEY GIVE ME INDIGESTION!" Ugly Cat yelled.

"What? But you were going to eat me!" said Pablo. "When you jumped on the paleta cart and hissed at me, I was sure you were fixin' for some mouse-meat fajitas!"

"EAT YOU?! I WAS TRYING TO RESCUE YOU! BIG MIKE WAS TRYING TO RESCUE YOU, TOO! YOU REALLY NEED TO APOLOGIZE TO HIM FOR YESTERDAY. HE WAS THERE UNTIL MINDY TOOK HIM AWAY. FOR YOUR INFORMATION, MY MOUTH WAS JUST WIDE OPEN BECAUSE I WAS TRYING TO TAKE A BITE OF THE COCONUT PALETA."

Pablo raised his little paw at Ugly Cat.

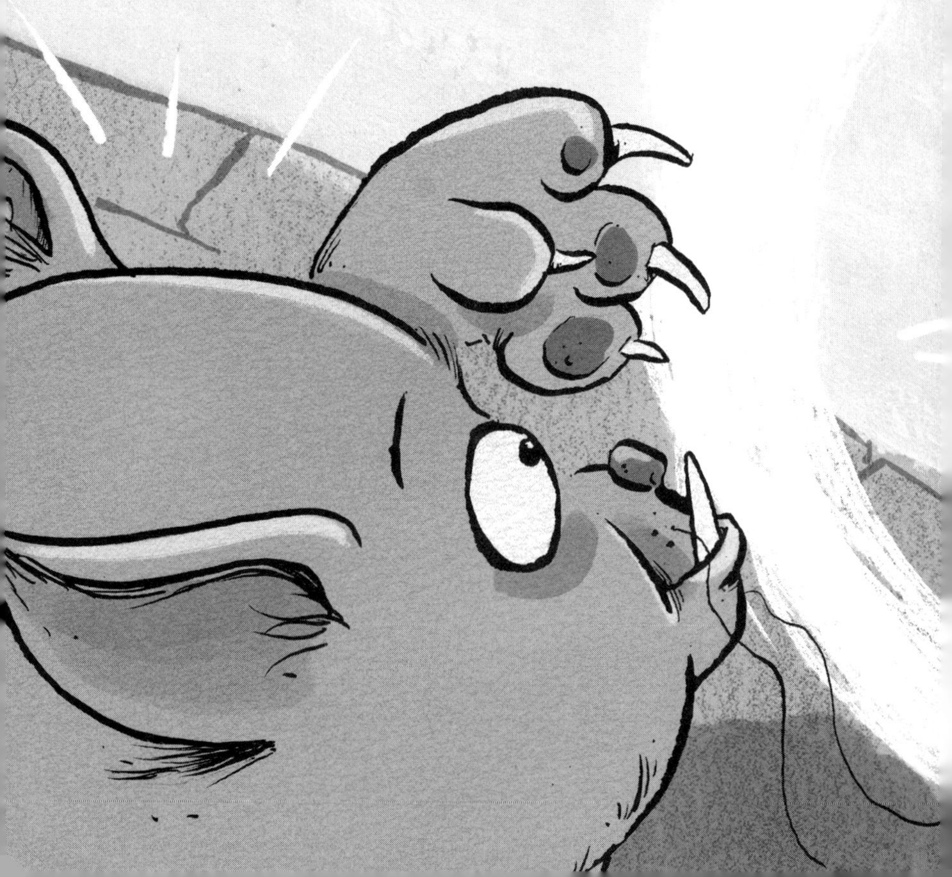

"You and your paletas! That's why we're in this mess. Eres malo, Ugly! I'm leaving!" Pablo calmly put on his hat and vest, plucked Ugly Cat's paleta right out of his paw, and then snatched his chicharrones. He stuffed his face with them.

"That's what you get!" Pablo said with his mouth full.

Ugly Cat took off running and crying.

There was a loud **HONK!** and a **SCREECH!** and then silence.

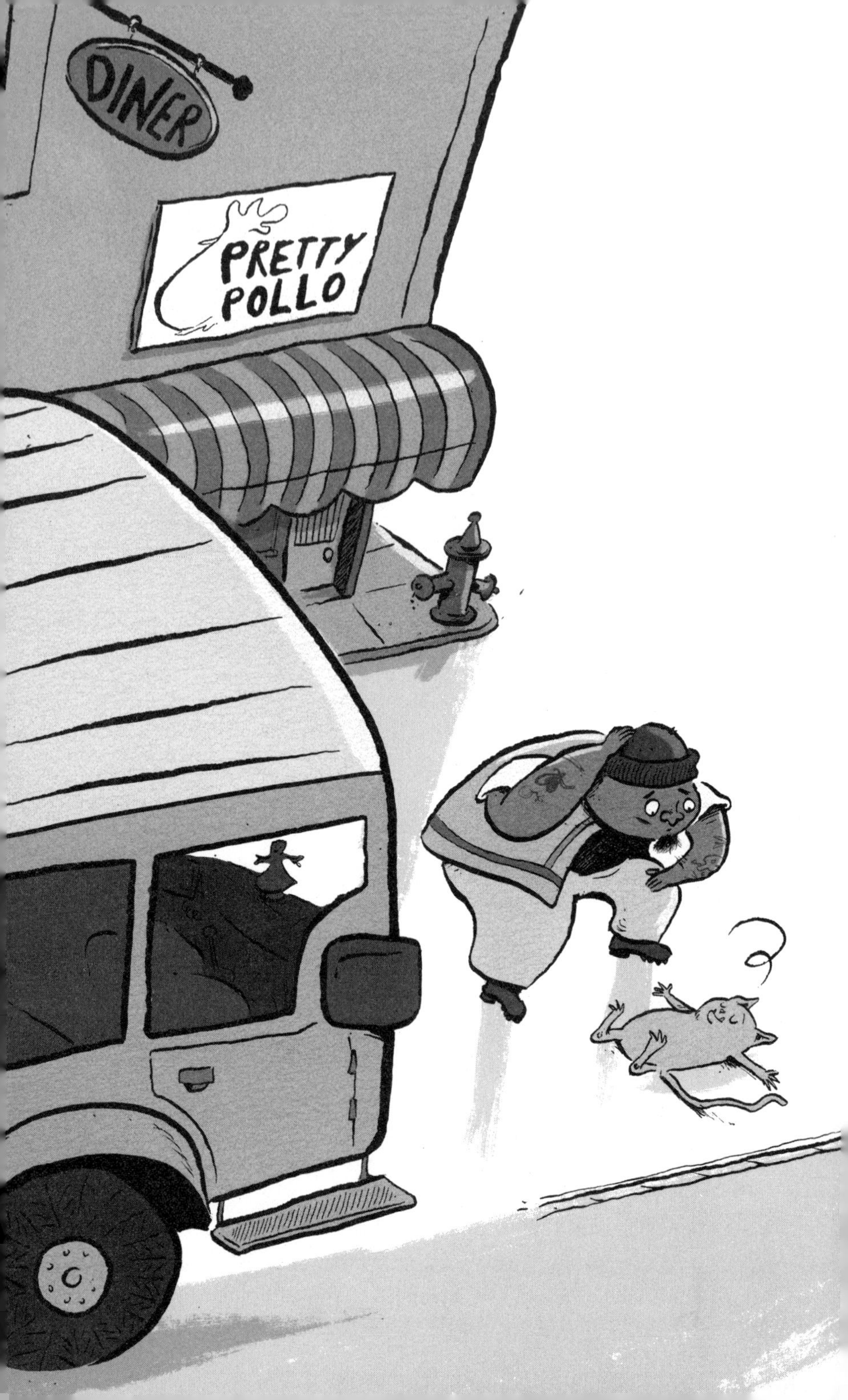
DINER
PRETTY POLLO

CHAPTER NINE

Another Little Misunderstanding

Ugly Cat, the sweetest and ugliest of all cats, had, sadly, suffered a fate too common among felines: death by truck. The worried driver of the garbage truck got out to check on the status of the truck. "**Dios mío! Poor little guy. I hope this wasn't the last of his nine lives**," he said. He gently picked up Ugly and put him on the sidewalk so nothing else would happen to him. Then, he hopped in his truck and drove away. Pablo watched as Ugly's orange tail swished back and forth and then stopped. He rushed to his best friend.

He kneeled down beside his friend, petting his head and crying, "Noooooooo! Por qué? Por qué, mi gatito feo? Why did you die? Ohh! You must have used up your other eight lives! Oh, Ugly! I am sorry I stole your paleta and your chicharrones! You can have

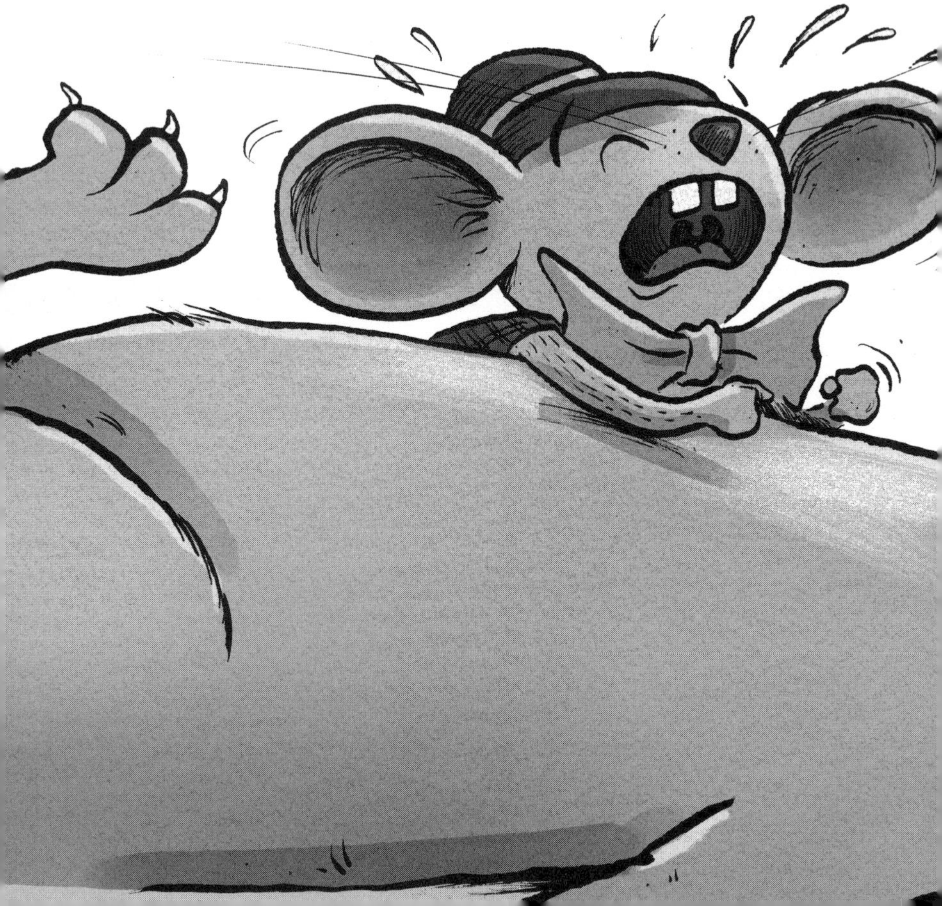

them back." He wailed, "Waah! Waah! Don't go into the light, don't go into the light!"

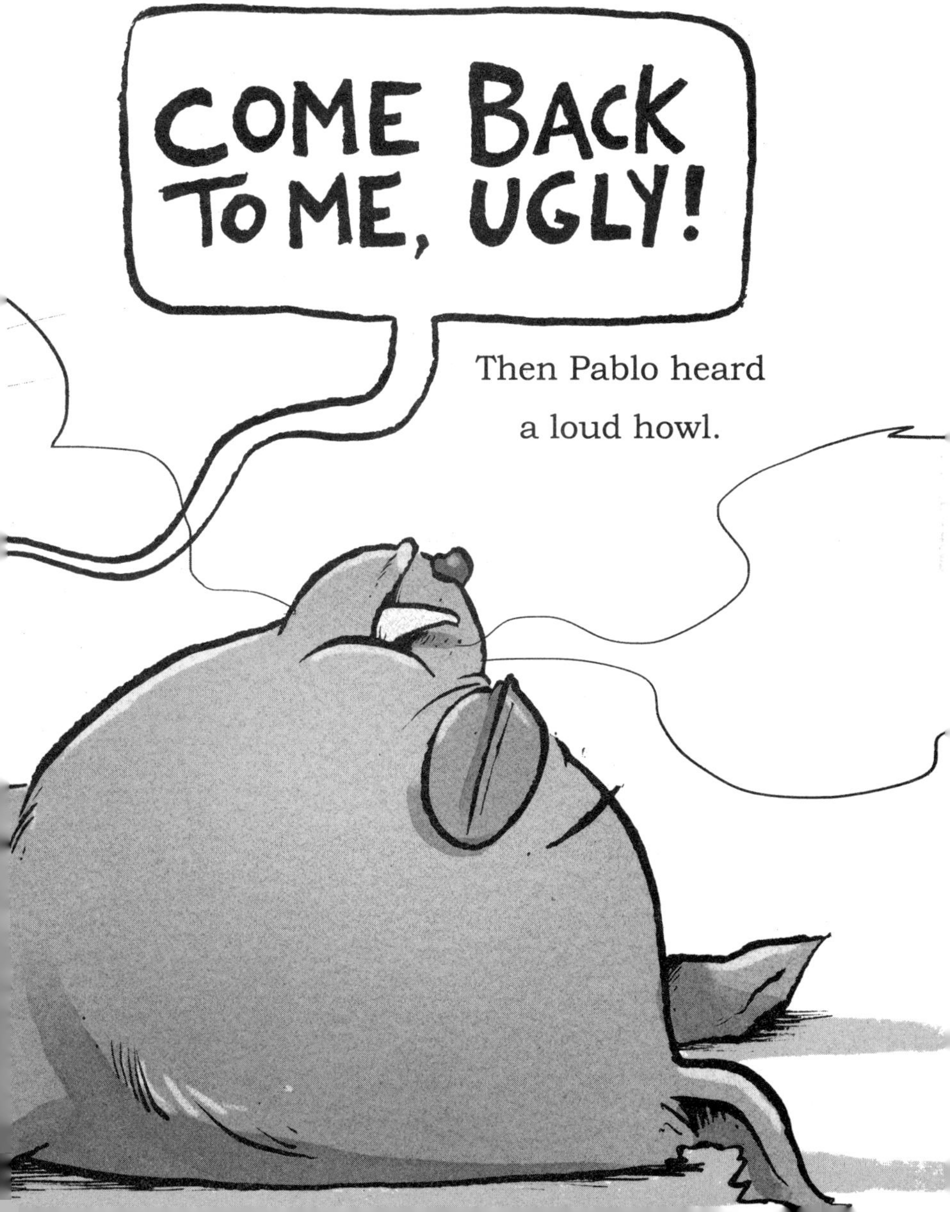
COME BACK TO ME, UGLY!

Then Pablo heard a loud howl.

"Ugly Cat! Mi carnalito! Why didn't you look both ways before you crossed?!" It was Big Mike. He had escaped through the hole he had dug under Mindy's fence to see if his friends had escaped the wrath of Snake Girl. He saw them run out of the park and chased after them only to find Ugly Cat lying in the middle of the road.

"Oh, Big Miguel, our Ugly Cat is no more." Pablo hugged Big Mike. Well, hugged him as much as a mouse could hug a dog. He rubbed his nose against him, and Big Mike shook the boogers and tears off of his paw. Pablo cried:

THIS IS THE WORST DAY OF MY ENTIRE LIFE!

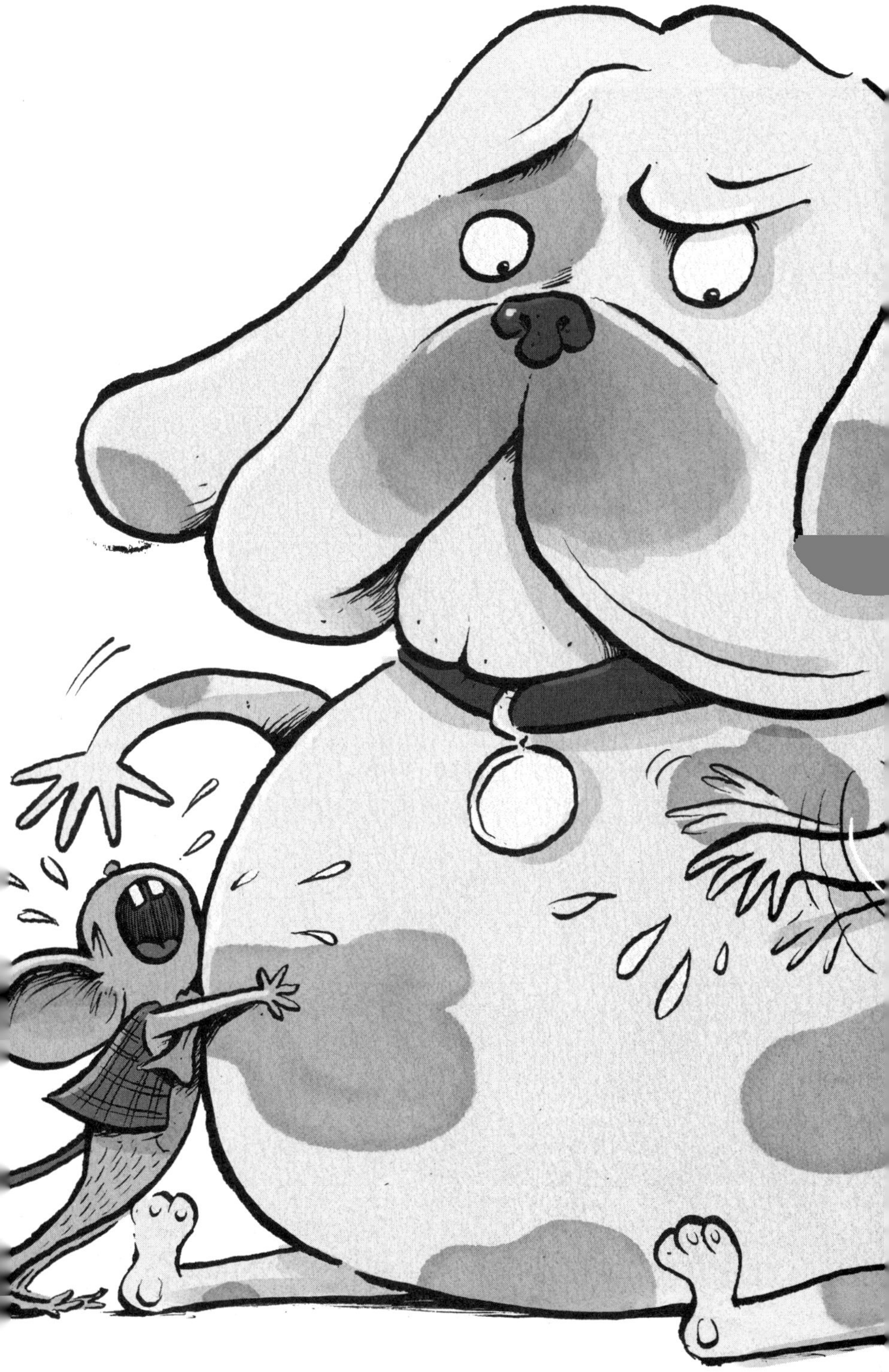

Big Mike pet Pablo on the head and said, "There, there, ratoncito. There, there."

"It's ratón, ratón, please, Big Mike. I know we are distressed, but there's no excuse for name calling."

Big Mike rolled his eyes and kept petting Pablo. "For someone who rode me like a bull after I said I didn't want to, you sure are picky."

Pablo sniffled. "I know. I know. I'm so sorry about that, Big Mike, so sorry. Before Ugly Cat left, he told me what you did for me. You are indeed what good friends are made of. Just like . . . UGLY! WAAAHH!"

Big Mike and Pablo talked about all the good times they had had together. About all the adventures they had been on. They began to cry harder.

"Oh, Ugly." Big Mike wept. "I really did forgive you for playing rodeo. I will miss you and your disgusting fur balls. I'll even miss your smelly tuna farts, because even though you always pretended that it wasn't you, I knew it was you. I mean, you're the only one in the neighborhood who eats so much tuna! But now, although the air will be a whole lot fresher, our hearts will be a whole lot emptier."

"Yes, Ugly. And I will miss your sweet donkey laugh," Pablo added. "Oh, how I loved to hear you laugh, Ugly! Even if it hurt my ears and sometimes woke up the neighbors."

Then, all of a sudden, they heard the soft braying of a donkey.

"Oh man, I miss Ugly so much. I can almost hear his laugh!" Pablo said.

Suddenly, Ugly Cat's body started moving. Pablo screamed and fell back on his tail. Big Mike yelped.

"A BURRO? I DON'T LAUGH LIKE A BURRO, PABLO!"

Ugly Cat was slowly getting up. And **TALKING**. This was impossible. They had seen the garbage truck hit the cat with their very own eyes.

Pablo screamed. "Ahhh! A zombie cat! Night of the living gatos! Someone get a stake! Big Mike, grab some garlic! He needs to go back from whence he came!"

Ugly Cat couldn't stop laughing. **"I'M NOT A ZOMBIE, PABLO! OR A VAMPIRE! IT'S ME— UGLY CAT, TU GATITO FEO! I WAS JUST FAKING IT. I LEARNED TO PLAY DEAD FROM THAT CRAZY POSSUM ON OUR STREET. I JUST WANTED YOU TO FEEL BAD ABOUT**

STEALING MY PALETA AND CHICHARRONES. AND IT WORKED!"

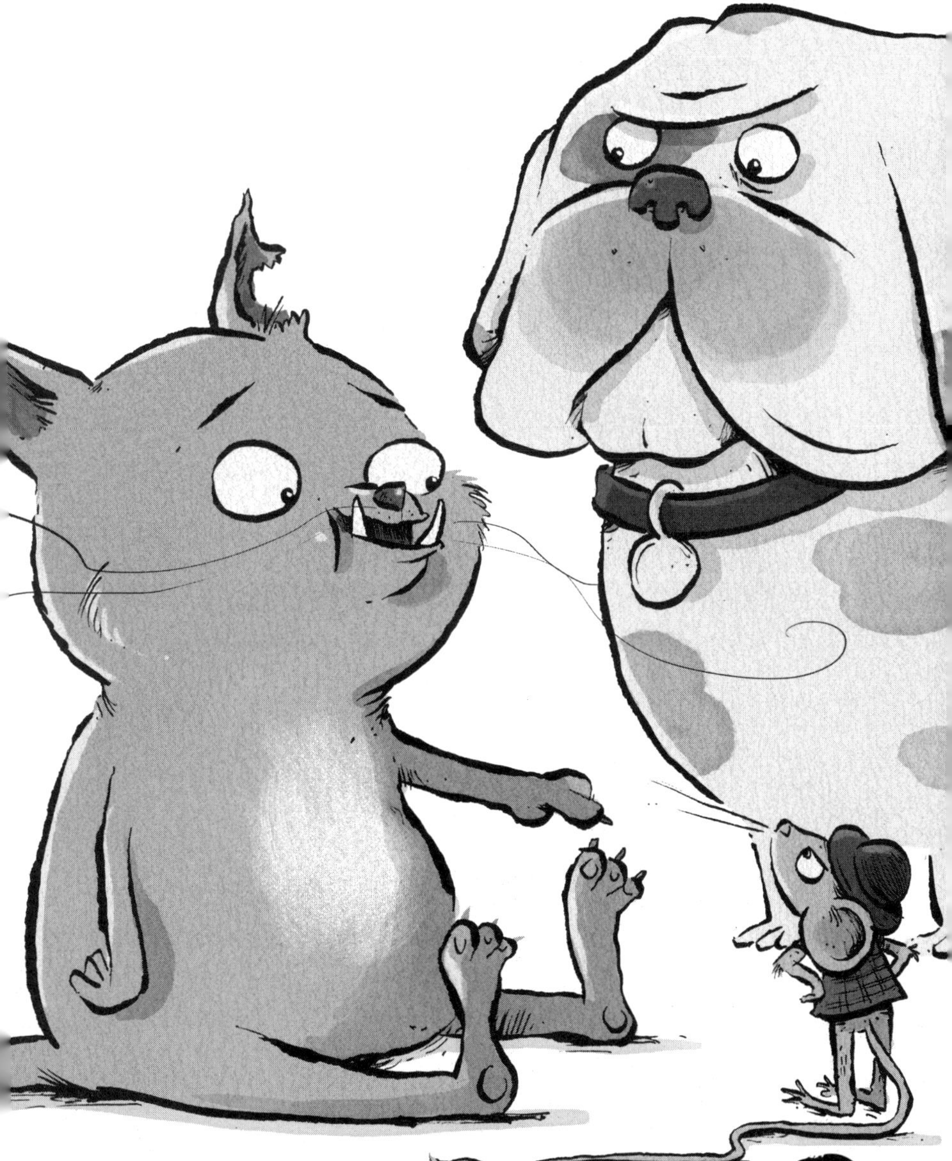

"What?! Oh my Gouda, I thought the truck hit you! UGLY! That was a super-mean trick! You even let us cry over your corpse, you . . . you . . . argh! I can't believe you're alive. First you try to eat me and then this!" Pablo turned to storm away, but he thought better of it. "Never mind, I don't care! I'm so happy you're okay!" Pablo embraced his friend.

"YOU'RE RIGHT, IT WAS A MEAN TRICK," said Ugly Cat. **"BUT, DUDE, YOU SHOULD'VE SEEN YOUR FACES! HA!"**

"What?" Big Mike growled. "We cried! That's not funny at all!"

Pablo scowled. "Big Mike's right, Ugly. We thought you were really gone."

"I GUESS YOU'RE RIGHT. IT WASN'T A

VERY NICE THING TO DO—EVEN IF I THOUGHT IT WAS PRETTY FUNNY."

"You two are unbelievable! What's wrong with you?" Big Mike exclaimed. "First the rodeo, then Snake Girl, and now this? I need a nap. I'm really tired from all this mouse lunch and zombie cat stuff." He walked away shaking his head.

"BYE, BIG MIKE, SEE YOU TOMORROW!" Ugly Cat shouted.

"PABLO, I CAN'T BELIEVE YOU THOUGHT I WAS GOING TO EAT YOU. I WAS JUST TRYING TO SAVE YOU, AND THEN YOU TOOK MY CHICHARRONES AND MY PALETA! MY PALETA, PABLO. MY. PALETA. YOU COULD MESS WITH MANY THINGS, MI AMIGO, BUT NEVER A CAT'S PALETA," said Ugly Cat.

"I know I should trust that your natural mouse-eating instincts are gone, but sometimes it's hard. I mean, look at me! Who wouldn't want all of this in their tummy? I'm a cat's dream dish! But, yeah, okay. I'm sorry," Pablo said. "Now, on to more important things: How about sharing some of your loot?"

"OF COURSE, MY HORSE! WHO ELSE COULD HELP ME EAT ALL OF THESE CRUNCHY CHICHARRONES? JUST MAKE SURE YOU KEEP YOUR MOUSY PAWS OFF MY PALETA," Ugly Cat said as he handed Pablo the bag.

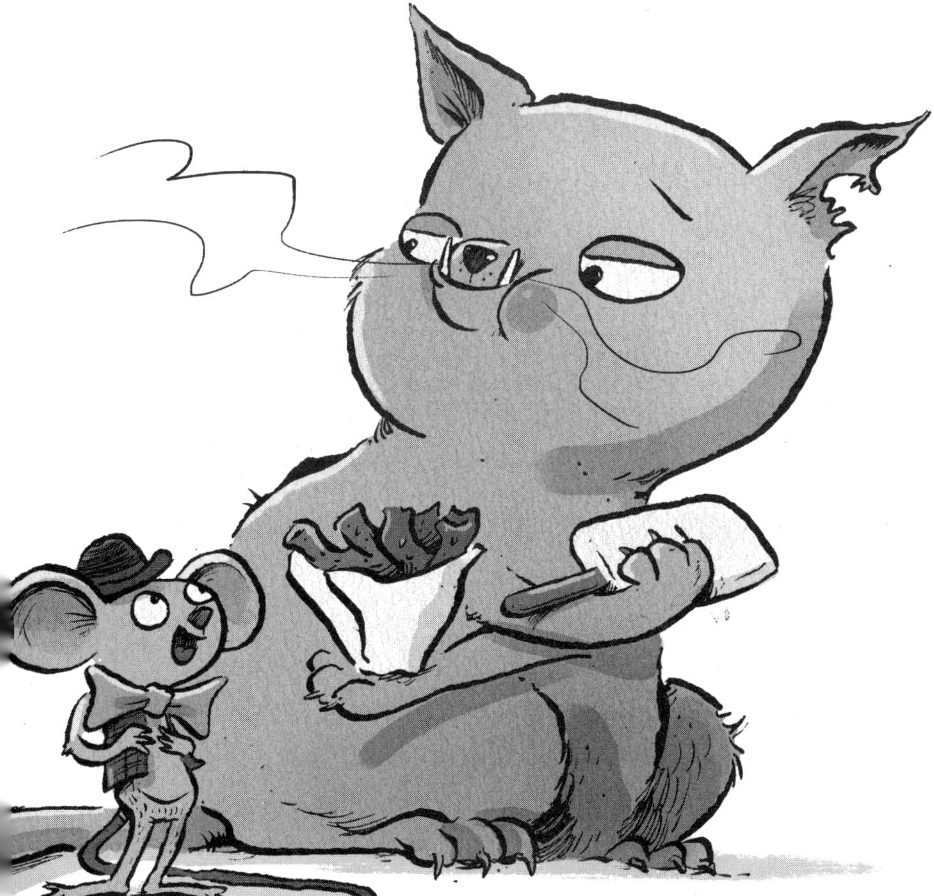

As they walked back toward Ugly Cat's house, the Mariposa Valley neighborhood dogs started barking, but the pair was too tired to pay any attention to them.

"HEY, WHAT DO YOU THINK WE SHOULD DO TOMORROW, PABLO?" Ugly Cat asked.

"Anything but the park," said Pablo. "Or playing rodeo. What about the zoo? Or the aquarium?"

"AS LONG AS WE GO TOGETHER. AND AS LONG AS THERE ARE SNACKS," said Ugly Cat with a smile. He tossed another chicharrón into the air and caught it in his mouth.

The two strangest and possibly ugliest-looking best friends laughed and ate as they walked past the barking dogs, all the way back to Longaniza Court.

Making sure to stay on the sidewalk, of course.

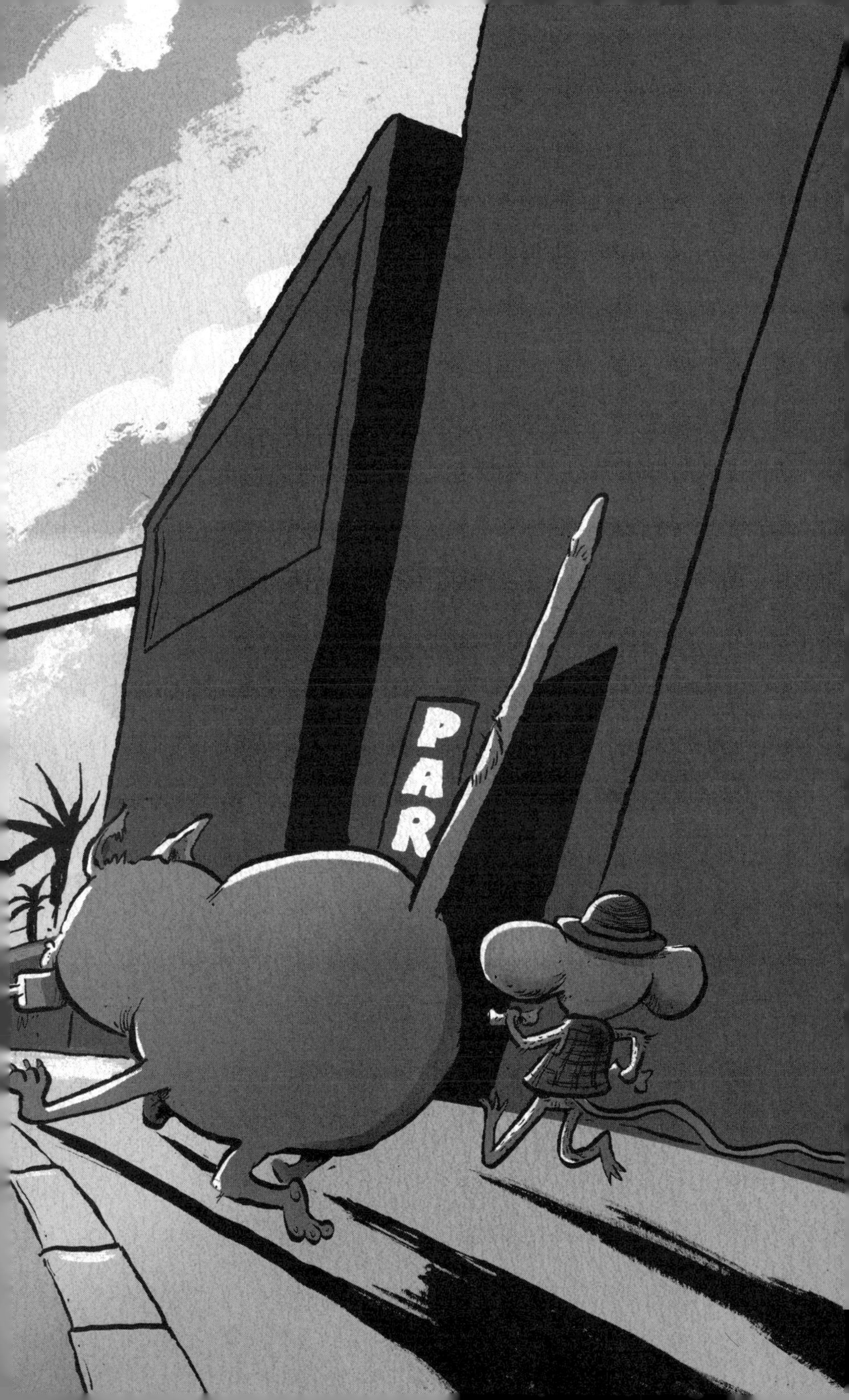
PAR

GLOSSARY

Abuela: Grandmother

Ayúdenme: Help me

Barriguita: Little stomach

Burro: Donkey

Chicharrones: Fried pork rinds

Coco: Coconut

Corazón: Heart

Dios mio: Oh my God

El parque: The park

Fresa: Strawberry

Galleta: Cookie

Gato: Cat

Gatito Feo: Ugly Cat

Limón: Lemon

Mi querido Feo: My dear Ugly

Mocos: Snot

Paletas: Ice pops

Paletero: Ice-cream vendor

Primo: Cousin

Qué la enchilada!: What in the world!

Raspados: Shaved ice

Ratoncito/s: Little mouse/mice

Salchichas: Hot dogs

Sandía: Watermelon

Tío: Uncle

Un gato tan guapo como yo: A cat as handsome as me

Vámonos al parque: Let's go to the park

Y listo: And done

RECIPE

WANT TO MAKE YOUR OWN PALETAS DE COCO?

Try this recipe at home.

Yields: 6–8 paletas

Supplies needed:

Blender

Popsicle molds*

Ingredients:

1 can of sweetened condensed milk

1 can of coconut milk

1 cup of shredded coconut flakes

½ teaspoon of vanilla extract (optional)

¾ cup of sugar (or to taste)

Directions:

1. Combine the condensed milk, coconut milk, and shredded coconut in a blender and blend until smooth. (Ask an adult for help.)

2. Add vanilla extract and sugar. (optional)

3. Pour the mixture evenly into each Popsicle mold*.

4. Insert sticks.

5. Freeze for 4 hours, or overnight if possible.

6. To remove, run the base of the molds under warm water.

*Tip: If you don't have Popsicle molds at home, use Dixie cups and wooden sticks.

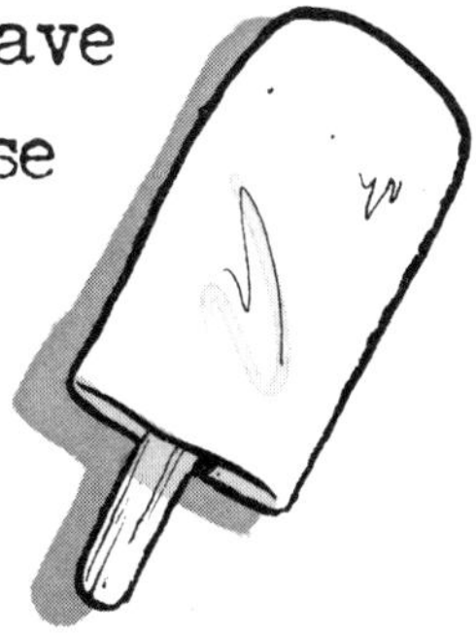

ABOUT THE AUTHOR

Isabel Quintero lives and writes in the Inland Empire of Southern California, where she was born and raised. Her debut novel, *Gabi, a Girl in Pieces*, was the recipient of several awards, among them the 2015 William C. Morris Award for Debut YA Fiction and the Tomás Rivera Mexican American Children's Book Award. For fun, she reads and writes, watches comedies, and eats paletas and chicharrones every chance she gets. Her favorite paleta flavor? Pues coco, of course.

ABOUT THE ILLUSTRATOR

Tom Knight lives on Mersea Island on the Essex coast of England. He was raised on a steady diet of Beano comics, Tintin books, and good sea air.

Stay tuned for more UGLY CAT and Pablo adventures in . . .

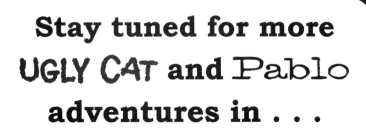

UGLY CAT & Pablo

AND THE MISSING BROTHER